TALLIEN
A Brief Romance

BOOKS BY FREDERIC TUTEN
The Green Hour
Van Gogh's Bad Café
Tintin in the New World
The Adventures of Mao on the Long March

TALLIEN

A Brief Romance

FREDERIC TUTEN

Introduction

Oscar Hijuelos

During the 1960s and 1970s, American letters bloomed under the influence of Latin American word-technicians like Jorge Luis Borges and magical realists like Gabriel Garcia Marquez. Since then, there have been micro-explosions of minimalism and recently - in the computer-generated writing age - a host of meta-novels. Thanks to the proliferation of writing schools in this country and despite reports of a waning readership, there generally has been a steady flow of highly crafted, technically proficient novels and short stories that are passed off, sometimes falsely so, as "literary" fiction.

Despite all the noise made about certain authors at any given time—as if fame equaled a true capacity to make literature—few writers have been consistent in producing works that are truly original or worthwhile. By original, I mean works that could only have emanated from the author himself or herself. If inspired writing is, in part, about "voice," and if voice is about an author's capacity to convey a unique personality while putting forth his or her vision of the world with all the aesthetic tools at his or her disposal, then few, to my mind, have touched the steady and innovative vitality found in the novels of Frederic Tuten.

One of these novels, *Tallien: A Brief Romance*, the book you are holding now, is something of a child born from quite different times. Frederic Tuten began writing it in about 1975 or so, a few years after the publication of his remarkable, critically acclaimed first novel, *The Adventures of Mao on the Long March*. *Mao* was a daring book that sparkled with wisdom, wit, and artistic insights. A novel of fragments that worked as a convincing and quite entertaining whole, it was, in its way, a work of genius and by far the best postmodernist novel to have come out of that period—one of our rare ages of reason in America. The Viet Nam war was just winding down. Protests, here and in Europe, were common and succeeding. Life, by way of social reform, was seemingly changing for the better. To have a leftist point of view was not to be in the hopeless and dismissible category it is today, and there was a sense of promise about the future. It *meant* something to be a citizen. Young folks felt empowered—by their passions, their beliefs, and the rightness of their convictions. And in those days, literature, in the hands of writers like Donald Barthelme, William Gass, and Frederic Tuten, was brimming with new life and energies. Old forms were being discarded; new ones were emerging.

In *Mao*, Tuten juxtaposes various texts drawn from history, literature, and his own invention, a method that takes its cue from modernist painters who incorporate found objects into their works (which sounds easy enough, but is extremely hard to do). The genius of the novel's organization, and the key to its success, lies with the author's unique and comic bent of mind. Although it features no overt first-person narrator, Tuten's choices of subject matter—revolution, art, and literature itself (including parodies of writers like Malamud, Kerouac, and Hemingway, among others)—speak distinctly about the author and his take on life and art. If there is such a thing as an autobiography implied by one's choice of materials, then *Mao* is the perfect example, as it could not have been written by anyone else. In my opinion, it stands alone as a masterpiece of its kind.

In his thirties when *Mao* was published, Tuten was a professor of literature and writing at City College, a working-class and immigrant "subway school" in Harlem. As one of his students, I spent many hours in his company, either in his small, florescent-lit office in a Quonset hut on the south campus, or in his Lower East Side walk-up apartment, where our class occasionally gathered. We were scruffy, quite hassled-by-life kids in search of ourselves, just making ends meet and much impressed—and reassured—by the trappings of Frederic's "crib." Contemporary art adorned the walls, including a lithograph of Chairman Mao by Roy Lichtenstein (which the artist created for the novel's dust jacket). Books rose high on shelves everywhere. Tuten's tastes were wide-ranging. He loved the works of European writers like Robbe Grillet, Ferdinand Celine, and Arthur Rimbaud but also held a great esteem for Mark Twain, Nathaniel Hawthorne, Dos Passos, Hemingway, James M. Cain, and Bernard Malamud, among others. The Europeans spoke to Frederic's sense of literary experimentation and to his romantic, confessional side. He admired the American writers for their sheer craft (as with Hemingway) and for the capriciousness of their voice, with Malamud and Cain being prime examples, in his view. I can remember Frederic saying that one of the finest opening sentences to be found in any novel was Cain's vernacularly phrased declaration, "They dropped me off the back of a hay truck about noon," from *The Postman Always Rings Twice.*

Tuten was one of the more impressive and accessible professors at City. He was tall and thin, with dark eyes and an angular, Italianate handsomeness to his quite expressive face. His long hair, cresting down his neck, and mod way of dressing—vest, open-collared shirt (at a university where most professors wore ties), corduroy trousers, and cowboy boots—seemed quite hip, circa the mid-1970s or so. Though he was a thoroughly literary creature, gingerly attending to the task of reading students' works and recommending books that we'd never heard of before (careful study of the texts and methods used in novels was one of his steadfast rules), the overall impression Frederic made was not so much that of a writer but that of a worldly artist, the kind of painter one imagined might have an atelier in Paris, a mistress or two in waiting, and the run of a bohemian life far more sophisticated and colorful than any of his students or our other professors knew.

Yet, for all his cultural sophistication and urbanity, Tuten always spoke about his Bronx working-class roots as if to say to us, "I am like you; we are cut from the same cloth." He had none of the prissiness I have since witnessed in many other writers; none of the amplified and self-glorifying ego that, from my observation, many a lesser writer wears like a badge of accomplishment and rank. His flamboyance and aesthetic demeanor, along with a touch of street wisdom and "chops," would have meant nothing, as kindly as he might have been to us, were it not for the great talent behind them. In writers' parlance, he was, and remains, the real thing.

There was, of course, a great deal of interest among us students about what Tuten would write as a follow-up to that remarkable *Mao* novel. I can recall his mentioning that he was writing a novel about Herge's comic-book character, Tintin, and seeing a chapter of the novel-in-progress published in *Fiction* magazine, circa 1976. Like a painter mulling over a series, it would take Frederic some years before that first chapter came to fruition in his wonderful *Tintin in the New World*, which would appear in 1993. But then too, at that time he was also working on something else, so he told me one day, a novel set during the French Revolution about a certain Jean Lambert Tallien (1767-1820). Tallien was a young man caught up in the machinery of the Terror, who, as a pro-consul appointed to preside over executions, fell in love, to his eventual ruination, with one of his doomed charges: Therese, an aristocratic Spanish beauty.

Now it happens that, as one who has always kept everything Frederic Tuten has ever published, I have a copy of *Tallien*'s first incarnation, which he gave me during one of my downtown visits with him. It is a preliminary and quite extensive story that came out in an anthology of experimental writing called *Statements*, published by the Fiction Collective in 1975. Its title, *Jean Lambert Tallien: A Brief Romance*, predicted that of the novel itself. Re-reading this story, I can see that, at first, Tuten was seeking to continue the technique he used in *Mao*, for this exploratory version was mainly a narrative compendium of found biographical details about Tallien, presented in quotations. (In interviews subsequent to the novel's publication, Tuten claimed that he originally got the idea for doing this while reading about Tallien's life in the 11th edition of *Encyclopedia Britannica*, which provided a brief summary of the obscure revolutionary whom he rescued from near-oblivion.) That early version also includes catalogue descriptions of antiquarian books, such as one finds in the novel, and delightfully stylized conversations among the characters. Some of Tuten's lines read like fragmented prose poems, as when Tallien first addresses Therese in prison: "In the dimness of this cell, Madame, you radiate. A glittering serene star, even in this dusky atmosphere." There are also somewhat straightforward third-person narrative passages, written in the elegant style of the period, that advance the progress of the story. Here too, as readers of this novel will discover, is included a modified tale by Washington Irving, set during the French Revolution. A wicked and ghostly story, this tale is reflective of Tallien's own sense of impending folly. Its hero, a bookish fellow named Gottfried Wolfgang, falls in love with a woman who has been beheaded on the guillotine.

Altogether, in its early, compressed form, *Tallien* is a flood of texts, imagined and gloriously written scenes, and conjecture. In short, it is a brilliant blueprint for what later became the novel and for much about the way that all of Frederic Tuten's novels are created, as the following passage reveals:

> "We tend to seek in literature mirrors or explanations of our Self, unless we skill ourselves to separate our own blood from another's *text* [italics mine]. This one sings dirges over his misfortune one day and makes rhapsody over his life-joys another....What have we to do with one another? Why these dreams and songs...?"

Such mirrors of the Self form an essential part of the beauty of *Tallien: A Brief Romance*. Though the novel is both a history and beguilingly tragic love story, it is also a book that tells two endlessly refracting stories. With the rise and fall of Tallien's romantic and worldly fortunes, his tale is framed by a subtle and mirrorlike narrative about Frederic Tuten's own past, a fragment of enticing autobiography. The novel is a quite moving portrait of father-son relationships, for in the telling of a tale in which a king is toppled during the French Revolution, it is the old leftist father, Rex, the union-organizer "king" of a family in the Bronx, found at the book's opening on his deathbed in a Jersey City hospital ward, who is being indirectly addressed by his long-estranged son. From the Bronx, the scene shifts to late 18th-century France. There, from the musings of a son who wishes, perhaps, to understand his dying father's inaccessible soul, readers are led in pursuit of a maddening and ill-fated love. It is within this framework that, to quote Frederic himself, "the story of someone who betrays the revolution and his principles" is told to Rex, "a person who has never betrayed his principles." This tender and elegiac scheme establishes one of the most engaging aspects of the novel: an air of personal intimacy that moves the heart and somehow moves the distant past to just a beat away from the present. Quite simply, one narrative seems the dream of the other.

The father's story, in and of itself, is worth a novel, but within Tuten's aesthetic of restraint, readers are given just enough information about Rex to sense his deeply held, Depression-Era-born idealism and its effect on his Red Belt-raised son, who, like the citizens of the French Revolution, wants to believe deeply that, as Rex says, "A new day will come soon...." Rex is a man who periodically abandons his family to pursue his boozing and John Wayne-type radicalism—his bills and his poverty, and the loneliness of his Sicilian wife Madelyn, be damned. In the end, Rex's greatest legacy to his son is his politics and idealism, but at what price? For the author, clearly exasperated by but admiring of the character he has created, this narrative is a way of putting his estrangement from his own father into perspective. Despite Rex's flaws as a family man, there is much wonderment in Tuten's sense of connection to him, as in this reference he makes to Rex in Havana:

> "At night, on the Malecon, he smoked fat cigarettes
> and looked out at the sea. Just as I did years later in

'58, with the lights flickering behind me as the city was at the edge on another historical platitude."

Aside from being a captivating look into the kind of personality who inspires so much leftist fervor in a son (and remember too that both *Tallien* and *The Adventures of Mao on the Long March* were written during a time of leftist ferment in this country), *Tallien*, with its vivid and dynamic narrative, seems to have as its underlying theme the capriciousness of fate and the strange workings of passions of all kinds—for social change; for a cause, unjust or not; for romance; for art; and for language itself.

Then, too, in this book's heart there is also a cautionary lesson about love. Yet, for the romantically imaginative and the artistic at heart, the pursuit of beauty and love, in any century, comes with its price. The feeling soul is destined, by the unpredictability of events and human nature, to certain disappointment. Paralleling such impossible pursuits of an object of desire—for example, in *Tallien*, the love of an emotionally opaque father or that of a 18th-century Spanish beauty—is the artist's own compulsion for extracting from, and giving form to, those inward musings that must, through his own arduous effort, be borne into this world. With this in mind, as I was reading *Tallien* again, I could not help but feel, as I do in reading all Frederic Tuten's novels, that the writer himself is the true hero of the book. For me, young Tallien, caught by the spurs of his own passion, harkens to the author-professor I met so long ago. I somehow feel that my passing summaries cannot do justice to the complexity of *Tal-*

lien or to the greatness of its language, which shifts seamlessly from Bronx colloquial speech to the florid constructions and rich vocabulary of an earlier time.

As a narrative, *Tallien: A Brief Romance* is in many ways straightforward; yet in many ways, it is not. The glorious—or inglorious—love-ridden tale, so lusciously told, moves far beyond simple and decorative exposition of details and events of history. Through its textural asides, this novel, in effect, is Frederic Tuten's way of allowing his readers to drop into that part of his consciousness, that corner of his thoughts wherein resides his own rich history, with its unique idealism and unique consequences. It is, in the end, a book that resonates on many levels; but it is Tuten's grasp of the fleeting nature and frailty of conviction that, in these particular times, makes it reverberate with a special irony. Conceived in the mid-1970s when our country seemed on the cusp of positive change, published in the late 1980s at the height of our rush into materialism, and now reissued in the new millennium during the second term of a presidency seemingly bent upon turning the clock back to an age of imperial conquests—in our wondrous, post 9-11 world, *Tallien: A Brief Romance* remains a fascinating and amazingly prescient novel, one that will stand as a reminder of better, more reflective times.

*****

TALLIEN
A Brief Romance

I

My father organized restaurant workers in New York City during the Great Depression. He was a Southerner, from Savannah, Georgia, born to a nest of thumping Bible-believers, though he himself, in spite of having had his ass whipped by my God-struck grandfather, blossomed into an atheist and a spiritual man. Like many Southerners, he was a rebel, and his rebellion took the tone, not of the outlaw cry of the Confederacy, which, in fact, he believed had the right to secede from the Union and to re-create itself an independent country, but of the rousing plaint of the "Internationale."

Renegade Baptist and radical, my father, Rex, was

held together with tight screws, two of which at least were buried so deeply into him that he could never find their points. He would never come to divine that his inflexible vision of right and wrong, of heaven and hell, of all manner of dark and light exactitudes, drew from the Baptist rod, and that his dream of universal justice, of a social heaven on earth, a paradise made by men and women inspired by principles of scientific reasoning, was extracted from the same religious nail. Hell was created by greedy men. Hell for the ones they exploited and twisted, and hell for the exploiters too, for in their greed they had lost the pleasure of their own lives; no matter how much they owned or whom they owned, they were lost to themselves because they could neither conceive nor allow a feeling of connection between their own lives and the lives of any humans unlike them—those who worked in factories, in fields, or who riveted the decks of large ships—nor could they trust or love their own kind, who, under the very law of dog-eat-dog to which they all subscribed, would do them in should conditions allow.

The camaraderie of the rich is built on the understanding that the hungry working world may one day grow so desperate that they will come, uninvited, and plunk themselves down in the wide capitalist parlors, their shoes soiling the carpets, their proletarian anger like a fine acid mist corroding the glossy mirrored walls and ungluing the reproduction Louis XVI armchairs and sofas.

"A new day will soon come, son," my father liked to say (in our little kitchen after coffee).

That was surely the day I, too, was waiting for. When would it come? Would the New Day abolish rent and utility bills, would it provide me with a second pair of shoes and land me a wholesome overcoat—one to put over the blanket in the freezing December nights of the post-Depression Bronx? (How rich to indulge myself in the anecdotes of childhood and adolescence! I myself would like to forget them, or trim them to smooth objecthood, freed from shame and the stink of poverty, and issue from my mind Pure Art, art with the human impurities removed—Me, the Bronx Racine, the Poussin of feelings, not one to be soiling the marble halls with childhood tracks. If only I had learned early how to operate the Neoclassical trash compactor, pressing and molding human experience into a manageable formal shape!)

Rex ran away from the military school where his father had sent him to become a man. Rex skipped out on the soldierly parades and the punishment marches and the mean things Southerners do to one another with their you-all smile. He joined his uncle in Cuba and smuggled cigars and ran rum through the Florida Keys. He learned to speak Spanish in Havana and he spoke it with a delicate Southern drawl. The ladies fancied that. (Would Thérèse— we'll get to her later—have fancied him, would she have daubed her Spanish lips with rose sherbet and read to him from Marx as the afternoon retreated from the Revolution?)

Rex played the dogs, drank little cups of incendiary black coffee, loafed about in the tangled gardens of small, family-style brothels where they poured him tall glasses of dark rum over shaved ice. Lost and won and lost at blackjack, his cards indifferent. At night, on the *malecón*, he smoked fat cigarettes and looked out at the sea. Just as I did years later in '58, with the lights flickering behind me as the city was at the edge of another historical platitude.

When and why Rex became a radical I still don't know, except for a few words left me on his deathbed in a Jersey City hospital thirty years after I had last seen him.

"Rex" (I envied the noble ring of his name), I asked, "you were a communist once, weren't you?"

"No, sir," he drawled, in that sweet, polite way white Southerners of his time affected when talking to well-behaved children and women.

(There he was at the tip of extinction, his body filled with painkillers to the edge of his eyeballs, him dying of cancer and emphysema, there he was, talking to me as if I were J. Edgar Hoover's son and not his. He was plying me with that smooth-talking charm he had spread on my mother when he was in the mood to keep her dreaming that one day he would carry her off from the Bronx sweatshops to the veranda of the Old Home plantation with the cotton and the honeysuckle and the plaid Dixiecrat wallpaper and the faithful black mammie who suckled him.)

"But, Dad," I pleaded, "how can you say that, it was the one thing about you that I was proud of all those years you were out there saving the world, and, Dad, I saw your Party card, the one Mom personally brought to the F.B.I. hoping they'd nail your ass down forever after you finally left us, you selfish son-of-a-bitch."

I would have given a lot actually to have said that, to actually have let him know right then when he was croaking and readying himself with big doses of soothing incantation ("I'm at peace with myself," and "I know I'm going to die, and I can look back and ask the Lord to forgive me for whatever I may have done wrong") that he hadn't put one over on me, even though I was sentimental enough to come by and say farewell before he went to join his Maker and give him a fraternal handshake up there in the Big Veranda in the sky.

"Well, Rex," I said, ingratiatingly, not wanting to ruffle him and risk the chance that, even though he had not mailed a postcard or phoned or sent me a fatherly word or one skinny dime since I had last seen him when I was ten, he might take affront and stop loving me on the spot.

"Somehow I had a crazy idea you'd been a communist," I meekly persisted.

"Well, son, that may have been, but I was never a

Marxist. They were throwing people and their be-
longings out into the street in those days and you had
to do something."

(Nobleman that he was, riding down the fields of
wrath, his terrible swift sword cutting a swath of fat
pinky-ringed capitalists, defunct leases and eviction
notices still clutched in their pudgy fists, Rex, the Radical Prince of the Confederacy, under whose ceaseless
guard none would suffer except his periodically abandoned family, unpaid bills rolling up like waves against
the door, his decade-old son staring up at the light
bulbs, waiting for them, like stars blinking off into
cold cinders, to go dead when the current was cut off
for failure of payment, his Sicilian wife, Madelyn, my
mama, humiliated by poverty, dying, literally, from
heartbreak and loneliness, her romantic pasta wilting
from neglect, Rex to the rescue!)

Never a Marxist! How lucky for me. How could I
have gone on worming through life knowing that he
might have been guilty of dialectical materialism, that
he might have tinkered, deep into the conspiratorial
night, with the theory of surplus value. This knowledge was a deathbed legacy. That father of mine sure
knew how to give his kid a lasting gift, something I
could go boasting around the block about, for, you
see, guys, unlike those fruity, brainy types, Antonio
Gramsci and Walter Benjamin, my dad was never
duped by fancy foreign theory. He was the all-
American radical, the John Wayne of socialism:

"Marshal, put down those folks' chair, nice and easy, you won't be needing it where you're going."

Perhaps it would have been better to dismiss him, to write him off as just another terrified poor soul who abandoned his family when things got too tough. But his glamour left me little room for that. Not that I thought so in the beginning, when it seemed a disgrace that he finally left us, but later, when manhood was fixing me up with the dream of him, trying to make a match of my fatherless self with the image of a father I could be proud to imagine.

I imagined Rex went to prison. I did not tell this when I was a kid, answering, when asked where my father was, that he was working in another state or that he was in the army. But I knew he was there, very far North, in the Siberia of jails, Dannemora, a real heartbreak house and no place to spend a Christmas, let alone three.

He wrote his wife, Madelyn, that she should forget him and get a divorce and remarry. But it wasn't in her. Besides, she was crazy for him in ways that are hard to understand today. Love had special allure for her generation, and sex had more power than it has today, raised as they were not to tumble into the sack unless they were married or told themselves they were *crazy* in love. And fidelity was part of the sexy package. It was the chain they snapped on each other just to feel the links in the night.

Anybody would know that by just listening to the

songs of their era—"Till the end of time, I'll be waiting for you"—and looking at the movies they loved
to get lovesick from. Good girls waited when their
men were away, bad girls didn't. Didn't Gloria
Stuart, in the role of the noble Mrs. Mudd, hang in
there bravely while her husband, the doctor, lan-
guished in a miserable, wet cell (*Prisoner of Shark
Island*), falsely convicted of conspiracy to assassinate
President Lincoln, and didn't the slut Ava Gardner
played in *The Killers* see from her faithless bed the
ceiling shimmy more than once while her lover, Burt
Lancaster, was serving slow time for grand larceny.

And then there was the double-edged Catholicism
and Sicilianness of the matter. Madelyn being both
Eucharist eater and spawned by a people driven mad
by the idea of honor. Or so Sicilians would like for-
eigners to believe. All their hocus-pocus, in fact, boils
down to a matter of stubbornness—like Gramsci's cit-
ing his Sardinian honor as reason for refusing to say
Uncle to Il Duce and Il Duce feeling bound in turn
to keep the Marxist ballbreaker tucked away in prison
safely writing his incomprehensible theories while the
real world went about its fascinating business.

Madelyn stayed pure for Rex and waited for him
to return. All the same, she had lost face: she had, after
all, married a man who wasn't a Sicilian. He wasn't
even an Italian, not even a Northerner from some-
place like Milano that might as well be Germany but
which could count, in a pinch, as Italy. And he wasn't
a Catholic. A Jew? *Magari.* Not even. Would that

she had been so lucky. Because, you know, in Sicily they've seen a few Jews, and if you come from around Palermo far back enough, you don't know if there isn't a little of the Hebrew in you, some Moorish as well, some dark-blooded stuff that sensibly hides behind doors in the thick afternoon blaze. You could look up Jews in the Bible. But this Rex came from the ice-bloods, Luther and Calvin, and where were they to be found in either the Old or the New Testament; they weren't even given a nod in the Koran.

What kind of church did he go to down there where he came from? It had no paintings or statues or soothing dark corners of altars, no candles, no holy water, no Communion or confirmation, and, especially, no confession. (So how did they rid themselves of sin?) What did his church have but a preacher, a man like any other who tumbled in the bushes with his young Georgia peaches as they rolled out of Sunday service? And what did this preacher preach but how terrible humans were, especially women, the polluted vessels, and how, no matter what good deeds humans did, God hated them anyway for being ugly and for being no better than spiders on His burning log, and that for no reason but His own He decided long before humans were even born who would go to heaven and sit by His generous foot and who to damnation, where hot pitch, a kind of roofing tar, was poured over them day and night forever and ever, even though they were pure and had done good deeds, and they would never know why they were made to suffer but had to accept that He had wished it—*Affari suoi*, His affair, as a Sicilian would say about a man whose business you better not ask too much about.

And he drank, Rex. Not like an Italian. Not like anyone in the whole Mediterranean world. You offer Rex a glass of wine before dinner begins. (This in itself is unusual, since wine is taken at meals, unless it's a small apéritif, or maybe a Fernet Branca if you've got a bad stomach and there's plenty to eat ahead of you, but you know Americans like their cocktails before sitting down to the meal and so you offer a glass of wine, red, homemade, very good and not like the junk from the store.) But Rex very sweetly and warmly asks if you have a whiskey of some kind, bourbon maybe.

Of course you don't have such stuff, who has it but mafiosi and other big-shot types trying to show how modern and American they had become. And Rex says that wine would be just fine, but you feel bad not to be a good host, so you offer him some brandy, which of course you keep in the house to serve on a special occasion like a wedding. Why, yes, he *would* prefer that, if you don't mind the bother. Then he starts drinking the brandy with a little water from the tap. And Rex drinks glass after glass of that stuff from the antipasto to the end of the fourth little cup of espresso, and then beyond even that until he starts singing "Dixie" and tells the story of Sherman's march to the sea, how that bastard Yankee burned everything in sight just for the pure mean feeling of the thing, just to humiliate the South.

Madelyn is clearly upset with him and is putting on a brave face and tries, as does everyone else at the table, to smile politely about the whole thing when Rex, in the friendliest way, asks why dagos crave to bow to painted plaster idols and when would they stand up as men and free themselves from superstitious papal enslavement and abject ring-kissing. The saving grace was that no one understood him, but when Rex launched into Mussolini, the whole family got the point.

"Now, that Benito of yours, he ain't half all that bad. He took the bull by the horns and went at it like a man, 'cepting that he got it all wrong and went and left his own class and brought the wealth of the people to the pockets of the *bouzuwazie*. Now, damn, it's time for the people everywhere to get off their behinds and stop being treated like niggers . . ."

Who was a nigger, my uncle demanded to know, the Italians?

Then it was really time to leave, my future mother says, and would Rex be so kind as to drive her and her mother back home, because it was getting late and they would have to go soon or they wouldn't get up to the Bronx before midnight, and at least for some people [laughs all around] there was work the next day.

Why, sure, and he'd be pleased to please her, as soon as he finished up his little brandy here, but, no, on second thought, just hold on there, Madelyn was right; they'd leave in a shake, then he'd drop her mother, the señora, home and then he and Madelyn could go off and have a nightcap at a little roadhouse he knew up around City Island. Where he was known, he might have added, because Rex was known in many diners and bars-and-grills and chophouses and homey little dives.

How do you organize a shop unless you talk to the folks punching the clock? He was great at talking to guys he was trying to get into the union because he didn't complicate the soup with foreign condiments, with German recipes and their Russian embellishments. So if he stepped into a bar, it was "Hi, Rex, have a drink," or "Hey, Rex, tell me when the revolution's coming 'cause I'm making plans to take the family for a vacation next month."

It's just as well for Rex the Revolution didn't come marching around the corner. He would have wanted to hang out with the other working stiffs and organize them against the guys who decided that unions were no longer necessary in the new socialist society, where, by definition, the workers themselves owned the means of production and therefore no longer needed a union to represent their own interests. If you are a sailor on the Tsar's *Potemkin* and you revolt, you're a revolutionary hero, but if you're stationed in revolutionary Kronstadt and you protest having your wormy rations halved, you're called a reactionary mutineer and a rabid anarchist, and the Revolution sends an army to cut you down like a greasy ship's rat surfaced on deck.

II

I would have liked to tell my father the story of the French revolutionary Jean Lambert Tallien. I would have told Rex of how Jean Lambert (1772–1820) was raised under a nobleman's roof, the boy's father the maître d'hôtel to the Marquis de Bercy, and how the marquis, according to the entry in an old encyclopedia, "perceiving the lad's ability, had him well educated."

Jean Lambert's father, the maître d'hôtel, had been trained to be efficient and invisible, the hallmark of good servants, and from childhood Jean Lambert, following his father's course, believed himself invisible, as well as one of the household implements, a kitchen knife, say, to be sharpened, used, and stored away. How he lifted himself from the back stairs and into the marquis's library is another story.

"Tell me," the marquis said one afternoon to the ten-year-old Jean Lambert, "what do you divine is the nature of woman?" "*Aimer, pleurer, mourir—c'est la vie de la femme*," replied the boy, to the pleasure of the marquis.

The marquis was a clever man and he delighted in extruding from the gray human stuff about him a form so animated and sparkling. Familiar with the enlightened theories of the day, especially the one claiming children susceptible to influences from the world about them, the marquis found in the boy the chance to test these ideas. Jean Lambert met the test. Indeed, in an epoch and place, namely eighteenth-century Paris, where wit and intelligence were regarded at least on a par with breeding and beauty, though naturally not on the level with wealth and station, Jean Lambert might have climbed several rungs above his circumstances.

But if he had had his way he would have abolished rungs and ladders, titles and classes. Little is known about Jean Lambert and how he came so early in his youth to his radical ideas and how he took it upon himself to write and print and post those incendiary placards. Perhaps as a child his father bundled him in wet rags and left him in a coal cellar overnight as punishment for some minor infraction—that would be enough to scramble the brains of some, impelling them forever to take the side of victims. Or maybe his feeling invisible pushed him to wanting to hear the privileged world squeak as he twisted the rope about its neck. All I know is that he took to virtue early on, and that he measured everything by the height of its virtue.

Jean Lambert was nineteen in 1791, when he left a clerk's job in a law office, a position with room for advancement, especially as Jean Lambert was under the marquis's protection, to become a printer's apprentice. What seemed so mad at first seemed more lunatic still when his father discovered that Jean Lambert was using the press at night to print inflammatory broadsheets—written by the youth himself—which he posted about Paris. It was shortly after the arrest of the King at Varennes in June of '91 when the most radical of his placards appeared, which drew attention to him by an elder revolutionary generation:

"Brothers! Citizens! Sisters! The King feeds his carps and jaded monkeys while Paris starves! Let our hunger and our anger be our strength! Sharpen your scythes for the Great Harvest. Ready your knives for the Banquet of Justice!"

What a hothead young Tallien was! Around him buffoons, clods, idiots, vulgarians, soup slurpers, calculators to the dime of pay to housecleaners; those who bark at waiters and insult chambermaids; sycophants of no special charm, toe-steppers at cocktail parties who neglect to apologize because you are of no particular power or fame; parasites who eat your dinners and bad-mouth you at another's evening table; idea horses, modeling the latest intellectual fashion, solemnity their cool façade—all these made their comfortable way in the Old Regime.

But Tallien was reckless, treating his youth and his passion for virtue as vastly expendable and replenishable capital. Tallien discounted his father's pleas to return to the law office and enjoy the comforts of society's blessing, and he persisted in flying from street to street in the dead owl of night, tacking up his wall posters on buildings and trees.

These wall posters, "of which the expenses were defrayed by the Jacobin Club, made Jean Lambert well known to the revolutionary leaders; and he made himself still more conspicuous in organizing the great Fête de la Liberté on the fifteenth of April 1792 . . ."

In organizing the now famous Fête, Tallien had distinguished himself for the overall scope and variety of activities as well as the niceties of detail appreciated by the crowd and the revolutionary elite alike. With austere joy Robespierre, the Incorruptible, noted from the reviewing stand (festooned with wreaths of blood-red roses forming the legend *Egalité, Liberté, Fraternité*) the plaster icons of the Revolution which Tallien himself had designed and commissioned; and Danton, who loved spectacles as much as he did banquets, took pleasure in watching a tree-high Greek temple of cake—Tallien's idea, which he had had executed, at no cost to the organizers of the festivity, by the Guild of Revolutionary Bakers—mounted on a flatbed wagon being pulled along the Champs de Mars by a team of young girls dressed in the costume of the nymphs of Reason. Even the ascetic Marat would have been pleased by the spectacle of fireworks had he been able to emerge from his soothing watery tub long enough to join the merry events, but Marat was suffering more than usual from his chronic skin inflammation and remained all that sunny day in his tiny apartment with its orange walls.

Without even meaning to, Jean Lambert had started to bake in the revolutionary oven and began to take on a recognizable shape, and not only in the cafés and clubs where dreams rose higher than radical soufflés bumping the roof of Paris.

Suppose you were, as was young Tallien, a rocketing star, saluted by butcher and perfumer and innkeeper, and suppose further that at the end of a lovely dinner, when you call for the bill, the *garçon* informs you that your meal, as well as any others you may wish at the present establishment, is free, its price already paid tenfold by the presence of its honored guest: you, that is, your own gracious self. Would it not be alluring to think yourself just that deserving person, you who had chanced danger and who had given yourself to the welfare of all?

"Hey, Jean Lambert, come over here! Look what I have for you, look at that, look at the clarity of his eyes and feel around the gills, such firmness. This fish was born to die for you. Take it! What's it going to do to you, swallow you? Don't be so stiff-necked!"

Jean Lambert was indeed flattered by the various attentions shown him, but his pride was such that he would have eaten a fist of paper and a cup of water each day rather than promote gifts for himself based on his fame as a revolutionary. He saw others in his circle pocket, shyly at first, small presents, and accept having favors done for them. He witnessed these same, who only yesterday denounced privilege and the corruption of bureaucrats and state officials, begin to take for granted these favors and gifts and express in obvious fashion their wish for more.

Others, he knew, were taking up residence at discount rents in the vast flats of nobles who had emigrated, and were having their clothes tailored, custom-made, that is, at rock-bottom prices. Some banked their loot in Switzerland. Victor Millet, nicknamed the Labrador because of his ability to pursue and fetch, to enter a nobleman's villa and return with a sack of gold pieces between his teeth, seemed to make the birthplace of Rousseau and the land of workable clocks his second home.

Meanwhile, Tallien's one suit decomposed in the natural way, buttons first, elbows and cuffs at a photo finish, breeches running second with baggy knees, and frayed seat coming in last. He got his clothes mended and patched whenever he could, not as in the days when he lived chez Bercy, where the staff under the maître's watchful eye kept Jean Lambert in tip-top shape, very much the gentleman if you didn't know his true circumstances. But he couldn't go there now, his father, even more than the old marquis, setting the tone for an inhospitable reception. It was the back door for Jean Lambert if he wanted to see any of his old kitchen-help friends or any of the mates of his childhood, for his father regarded him as a species of traitor, an ingrate who was biting the sweet hand that had fed him. What evil indeed had the marquis done him that Jean Lambert behaved this way, raging against his betters and using the very skills of writing taught him under a nobleman's roof to demand the King's, a nobleman's, head, to demand that the world turn upside down so that beggars with greasy underwear might mouth imbecilities about the rights of man. The right of a man, shouted Tallien père, is to jump off a bridge and hang himself when he starts putting on airs and thinking he knows more than the deity who created him.

The marquis, when Tallien wrote asking to visit him, returned a message, delivered by hand to the revolutionary's tiny, top-story room, which said: "My dear boy, illness in itself should be no reason to put away the chance to receive a friend, but an illness such as mine feeds on sorrow and worsens on what it feeds. Allow me, if I may be permitted, to recall, in solitary, unjolted memory, the tenderness of your face (and the tender days of another era so far away in human history, if not in actual historical time) when I last beheld it."

It was a killer, that letter. How long did it take him to compose that little dart, Tallien wondered. It was really good, looked like a little nothing, then it went sailing off and sped deep into the heart. The marquis's door was closed. Henceforth, there were no fathers, no mentors. The Revolution was his home.

III

Louis de Saint-Just was twenty-seven when executed; Georges-Jacques Danton, thirty-five; Maximilien Robespierre, who did in the latter (as well as many others), hit thirty-six; Camille Desmoulins, Robespierre's schoolboy friend, went raving to the Machine at thirty-four; Jean Paul Marat had attained the giant age of fifty when Charlotte Corday stabbed him cleanly in the heart. And she was twenty-five when the Revolution parted her head from its trunk. Louis XVI, whom much of the fuss was about, was decapitated and thrown into a lime pit at thirty-nine.

Many died even younger, as saplings, the sap still

flowing richly. They would have been happy to live a few decades longer and enjoy the green figs of spring. Imagine the sweetness of France in 1792, '93, '94, and even 1795, if you had your health and a little money in your pocket and no one had orders to cart you off to prison. Ozone still sheeted the atmosphere and the clouds and sky were crisp. Crisp, too, the vegetables and fruits, which were small and hard and incredibly sweet. You could take a girlfriend or even your wife and family for a day in the country, as far as the Château de Vincennes, or the Parc de Saint-Cloud, if you preferred the other direction—who cares what direction, so long as you are out there, the sky full and the air warm and slightly breezy, and you and yours are lying under the vast foliage of a vast green tree, a glass of new wine (made with no preservatives or chemicals or coloring or wine flavoring) nuzzled by your thigh, your eyes shaded by the loving girl leaning over you.

You look about, you who have scorned Church and its exploitation of the spiritual sentiment, its turning the joy of life into a castigating mumbo jumbo, and you say, "God! What a day!" You would like to kiss a tree and embrace the astonishing earth and give your total thanks to the Supreme Being; you could almost believe, as Robespierre in public countless times professed to believing, that "Nature is the true priest of the Supreme Being; the Universe is his temple; virtue his cult."

Later, a little tipsy, you carriage-ride back to Paris. Your girl's hand in your crotch and yours in hers. Her bodice is slightly open and her breast sways with the gentle sway of the coach. Boucher himself could not have painted a nipple as beautiful as hers, that blush of reddish pink inching above the cut of the cloth as the coach lurches and sways. Okay, so what if old age is ahead of you, it hasn't arrived yet, it's still ahead and far away; so the teeth will rot and leave baby stumps and you'll need a hoist to raise your cock when, before, it would jack up all by itself at the sight of a creamy neck, so what, let it come. But for now there's the ride and the whole of Paris still miles away. And your own death still further ahead, too far away for you to see it or to allow it to depress or frighten you.

Who would not have wanted to stave death off just a bit longer? Imagine how tough it was for them to have to say goodbye (when there was still time) to everyone while the Revolution was still in full flower, and you were filled with curiosity, as you naturally would be, to know what will happen next and whether the Revolution will carry and jump forward and what new and surprising things it will usher in. Who would have thought even then, as the tumbril is bringing you to the Place de la Revolution to have your head lopped off, that the use of the *vous* would be abolished and everyone addressed in the comradely *tu?*

It was Jean Lambert Tallien who helped many on their way to the next world. Not that he was the executioner himself—that job had been spoken for from one generation to the next within the same family, a hereditary position, a father-to-son trade. Tallien used his rhetorical arts to ensure that the King and his sister, the Queen and her son, the aristocrats, their supporters and their suspected supporters, the counterrevolutionaries, the weak-kneed, the less-than-a-hundred-percent for the policy of the ruling faction —the Jacobins led by Robespierre, his brother Augustine, Marat, and Saint-Just—would have their worries ended once and for all.

Some cases were clear-cut. A man was found with documents proving that he was in the pay of the Austrians to broadcast rumors that the revolutionary leaders were accepting money from the English, to whose country they would soon flee, leaving the people to be massacred by the invading Prussians. Another, a woman of nineteen, in the guise of a delegate from the commune of Saint-Denis, was discovered to have modeled herself after Charlotte Corday and had for her target no less than five of the leading revolutionaries, including Tallien himself. For him, according to letters found on her person, she had intended a shower of sulfuric acid for his face and eyes.

No one who has not lived through a revolution can know or can believe the amount of stinking sheets hurled against it by a variety of antagonistic arms. The counterrevolution tries to corrupt the revolutionary leaders through direct bribe and promise of a high position in the Regime to be restored, or they are asked to pretend to keep their place in the Revolution while actually slowly deflecting it, turning against it in the very name of the Revolution itself, and by this route send to their deaths the most honest of the Revolution; or the Old Guard are given financial and military support to provoke or maintain a civil war and are paraded to the world as men of principle and of solid values, while the revolutionaries are pictured as mad dogs who can't even keep their checkbooks straight, let alone run a nation's economy, mad dogs to be put down, shot, poisoned, bludgeoned behind the ear. That's for starters, the appetizers, so to speak, of the greater and more subtle menu of endeavor yet to come.

The counterrevolutionary banquet—as enticement to betraying the Revolution—comes in many varieties: some are patently close to eating orgies and lack refinement; others are in the dietetic line, offering up a cup of water and a few steamed vegetables. This course has great appeal to the Spartan and health-conscious, the high-minded, who find in it the measure of their wish to keep the goals of the Revolution lean, like their own svelte selves. Jean Lambert seemed to have no appetite for the banquet, lean or fat, and he was thus chosen by his comrades to keep an eye on the shop when someone had to go to lunch or take a leak. Sometimes at night when he'd come home from a day at the revolutionary tribunals, his head would spin from all the stories and the pleadings from those tried. He'd stretch himself out on his cot and try to sleep, but instead he would review the day's proceedings.

I don't think it would have been different had he lived in our times and clicked on the TV with the hope of drowning himself in a game show, "Wheel of Fortune" or "Jeopardy," let's say. Chat programs with lively hosts and witty guests ready to talk up their latest enterprise might have held his attention for a few evenings, but I can't imagine for longer than that. Of course, if he had cable TV, he could turn on the porn shows and wank off, as the British used to say, into his sheet or an old towel. He might have liked the show where ordinary folk, housewives, as they were once called, did a striptease and jiggled their tits under hot lights. The Revolution frowned upon prostitution as a vestige of the former order, and Tallien wouldn't be caught dead in a whorehouse or behind a stall with a *poule* for an old-style quickie. He didn't seem, at this point, to have many girlfriends, and he wasn't going steady with anyone, that much is known. So that's why I go into this wanking-off business, because the economy of the thing makes sense when you think of the trying day he spent having to hear, as I've already mentioned, all those stories and pleadings.

The clear-cut cases were no problem. For those, "the blade," Tallien would say, with uncharacteristic brevity. But at times it would take some thinking about. Instance: Jean Moelle, assistant baker, age twenty-two, from the bakery where they make those famous guillotine pastries that were so popular not so many weeks ago. Hearing how great these cakes are, an agent of the Committee of Public Safety goes to the bakery just to buy a cake or two to take home to show his kids. The shop is a little out of his way and so by the time he gets there he's a trifle pooped and overheated and, well, let the record show, a bit irritable.

"Citizen, I'll have two of the Machine," the agent says on entering, obviously not noticing that there is a little queue. Those things happen, and no harm is meant by it. But this Citizen Moelle calls out from behind the counter: "You wait your turn, you. This is not a stable where you whistle to your horses, eh."

"And who would take you for a horse, you with the face of an eel?" the agent replied coldly.

"And you with the face of a [here the baker spoke the word very softly] prick, you prickface, get at the end of the line and try to control yourself before you piss in your pants." The agent had the common sense to let it go and to pass it off as a joke, so he went to the back of the line and started chatting with the customers—obviously, this was his way of keeping face. But this Moelle, the success of his repartee gone to his head, now starts shouting, with the shop as his audience: "Before, at least, there was respect for things. Little shits didn't just go around barking orders. Now everyone is a boss."

The agent says he let this pass.

"No one wants the old times back, let's agree on that. I say, let's agree on that!" [Here, coughs and voices of approval from the line.] "But in the old times rank had meaning, not like today when any fop can put his oar in the soup of the people."

"Enough of that now, you've said more than too much," the agent shouts from the end of the line.

"That is not for you to say, monsieur. I'm a free citizen and say what I wish, and when that is no longer allowed, I'll stop baking these little head-choppers and really do something to make heads roll."

All this ambiguous hot wind brings the baker to the Tribunal, arrested for inciting the people to rise up against the Revolution. The baker does not deny he said these words but claims they were misrepresented by his accuser, the agent, who was a pain in the ass and wanted to make trouble just for spite. So now what? The case is made that, with the counterrevolution at the frontier, no one can be permitted to speak without thinking of the consequences, and certainly not be allowed to shout provocative words to inflame or alarm the public or to cause it to distrust its leaders. How this windy injunction applies to this blowhard of a baker Tallien must take a long leap of the imagination to comprehend, and he would just as soon dismiss the case, but there is the consideration of the agent's reputation; as a representative of the Republic, he cannot be made to look like a fool at so serious a moment when real reactionaries lurk about sowing discord.

So the baker gets a few years to stew in the tropics. He must be used to the heat anyway, the great Danton quipped, having baked all that bread and cakes, and he won't come back much worse for wear, if the fevers don't carry him off.

The baker's case was a sad farce, and it was lucky for him that it ended as well as it did. Not that Tallien took the outcome that lightly. Deportation was a heavy stone for the baker to swallow, but some good would come out of it in the long run, a lesson in the correctness of revolutionary demeanor in revolutionary times.

There was a more haunting case, one that played in Tallien's head for many nights after it was over, and made him wonder about the course of the Revolution.

(I lived a notch or two below the Red belt of the Bronx. I grew up with self-educated workers. Communists. Eastern European Jews, mainly. Furriers, restaurant workers, mattress makers, shop stewards, union organizers. They believed that reading was power and they encouraged their children to read and become powerful. In their early teens, my friends were already poring over little, thin, blue-covered editions: Stalin's *Dialectical and Historical Material-*

ism; Lenin's *On the Woman Question*, Engels's *The Origin of the Family, Private Property and the State*. I was in a fog of enchantment with Catholicism and very much disturbed and much in awe of these young Marxists. It was from them, not my father, that I learned that when you boil a pot of water, at first you don't see the bubbles, but they are brewing none- theless, and they are undergoing a quantitative change to—*violà*! the bubbles—a qualitative change. That was the essence of dialectical materialism, which ex- plained in some way the revolution that would one day violently bubble forth in America. And from where else but my street pals did I get the idea that property was theft? If you owned great amounts from another's labor, you were a big crook; if you owned a little from another's labor, you were a small crook; if you owned from another's labor, you were, let's face it, some variety of crook. My mother hated my friends and didn't want me near them, because they were "godless materialists." She was right. That's what they in fact were. It shocked me that they didn't believe in God. Only animals, unknowing beasts, didn't.

When I was thirteen, I had a long talk with Eric, the one who killed himself a year after Khrushchev's revelations about Stalin at the Twentieth Party Con- gress. [Leave it to Eric to have discovered the most painless, scientific means of doing himself in, CO, through a tube in the floor of his car, the very Plymouth he used to transport his commie leaflets from the Bronx to Manhattan.]

"Man was created by God and has a soul," I declared.

"I believe that man is simply an intelligent animal."

I denied that man was an animal. The idea was degrading.

"Is he a vegetable?"

"Of course not."

"Is he a mineral? Like a stone."

I was in his net.

"Then," he said, "what is left?"

"Those are just words, a human's classification. Man seems like an animal but is something different from an animal."

And we went back to the business of the soul again, because that was my strongest, and the most irrefutable, card in my hand. The soul, as is obvious to anyone who possessed one, I explained, suffused the corporal self. It was invisible; you could not cut it with a scalpel. It was immortal; and to deny its existence was perverse and brutish. Eric's sneer incorporated the history of the struggle for the acceptance of Darwin's theory of evolution and Marx's analysis of the narcotic function of religion; it was a marvelous pitying smile for the poor benighted schmuck who was me.

I wonder whether, years later, the tube in the car, the odorless, tasteless gas bubbling in his bloodstream,

the cells and the tissue just eating it up and Eric fast
becoming dead, soulless meat, he might have thought
that, along with the shattered illusion of socialism and
the glorious myth of Stalin, so, too, went the myth of
the spontaneous creation of the universe. Did the pain
of disillusionment imply the possible existence of a
spirit, invisible and immortal? Did he ask himself, as the
last cell in his brain croaked giddily, where in the material matrix came the spiritual capability of the human
to suffer for ideas, as he was doing right then? As he
had done all his youth. Just to have toted those banal,
boring leaflets from borough to borough for so long!
And in the fifties yet, when the F.B.I. was living in
your jockstrap and liberal intellectuals were frying
communist Jews for their prose style. Eric, I admire
you for having had the crazy balls to believe anything
so deeply. [And prouder am I still of your ability to
take so hard your having kept, against all reason, the
faith with a fortress you had never seen and its mus-
tachioed commander you should have known was too
good to be true.] Even as I'm writing, slimebags walk
the earth who wouldn't give a hair from their toe
for anything they can't feel, eat, screw. They'd rip
the tusks off every elephant on earth and personally
brain 'em with the bloody stump if it got them a two-
bedroom condo in a quality section of Manhattan.
Eric, imagine what they'd do to the Third World just
for the promise of some oceanfront property on Long
Island. Eric, you poor sap, they are the real material-

ists. You just the Byron of the dialectic. Only those capitalists of '29, who threw themselves out of skyscraper windows in mad longing for their nest eggs which had preceded them down the chute, do I respect as much as I do you. Like you, they, too, were faithful to their ideals. Pure materialists braining themselves on the pavement, true to their belief in the lifegiving potency of wealth. Salute, comrades.)

Paris was heating up. Fear and anger, one generating the other, shouldered through the streets. You could walk out for a loaf of bread with the intention of returning home in a few minutes, a half hour at most, unless the queue was long or the bread had been sold out before the normal time, in which case you would have to find another bakery, but let's say that today everything was normal and you left your flat and went out into the street. Now you are turning a corner and, wham, you smack into a knot of people beating someone up. They're giving this guy jabs and punches and hard kicks. His nose is bleeding and his hat is in the mud. All you want is to pass by and get to your bakery without a hitch, but someone shouts to you, "Hey, citizen, give us a hand with this aristocrat, he won't let us take him to the police."

What are you to do? Are you going to say what you feel: Look, take your aristocrat and stuff him up your nose, I've got a life to get on with, so let me pass! You know you're not going to say that and you know you can only hope that with all this commotion the police will arrive first, because you don't want to go all that way to find them, following behind the little crowd like an excited dog, and waste the whole morning. What would happen, say, if in that little crowd someone decided that you were not aiding, when asked, the cause of the people? What would you say when charged with avoiding revolutionary responsibility? Or perhaps a worse charge, that of being a secret sympathizer with the Old Regime, of wishing to bring back the whole mess of powdered wigs by letting this spy get out of the people's hands. What would you say? That you had no time to help because you were afraid the bakery would run out of baguettes!

A criticism could be read into that simple statement. That was exactly what the counterrevolutionaries were saying: while there was want under the King, under the Revolution there was nothing. You can hear the prosecutor barking at you in the dock: "No bread! Are you saying that the Revolution allows the people to go without bread? This is calumny and alarmism, at a time when our armies are fighting for our freedom and our lives against the invading butchers of the White Terror." So you shout back: "Of course, I'll help, citizen, let's drag the bastard to the police by the balls if necessary." And you throw in a punch or two yourself, just to be sure it's on the record.

Tallien imagined that that is how it happened. One

day, a leftover from the time before the season of hope
and miracles took to the street for a walk. His clothes
were shabby but clearly belonging to the lower nobility or some upper order now defunct. He didn't walk
like a regular person. His back was too straight, his
head too erect, his movements too fluid. And he was
very tall, always a sign of some high-born type. Under
his arm he carried a beautiful green leather case. It was
really beautiful. Tallien saw it and longed for it, the
leather so soft, worked in Morocco, probably Fez, and
its color the color of a parrot's green wing or of a
young pistachio, green from its shell.

(That green went well with the green of Tallien's
eyes and with the black of his long hair. Thérèse—
we've still to come to her—once told him that, when
she first set eyes on him in the dim light of her cell,
she mistook him for a prince she knew as a child in
Spain, because he, too, had carried such a green case.)

He was walking along, this distinguished-looking
man, passing through a street where he was not
known. In Paris then, every new face raised curiosity.
So when he passed by the open door of a printer's shop,
his green case flashing like a green rectangle against
the flat surface of the day, the master printer, Citizen
André, who was lounging over a morning beer, sees
him and calls out, "Green, green, the color of my
hopeful disposition." Don't think that this citizen
made that up on the spot, because he didn't; like many
printers, he read a lot of the material he was to set up

for the press, and he had a wide range of references to cite and to show off when he was in the mood. (You could probably trace his line to something he had once read and recited to impress a girl who wore a green ribbon or bow.)

And because Citizen André had read so much and spouted it off at every chance, and because he carried himself with an ironic swagger and always had some sharp political remark to make at the expense of anyone alive or dead, he was elected the section leader of the commune of his district.

Now the man with the green case raises his hand in a wave of salutation and continues walking. The printer doesn't like him. It's as simple as that. He feels that in that wave of salutation is a patronizing wave of dismissal. An unfriendly and unrevolutionary wave from a man too much in a hurry. When you want insults, you find them everywhere.

"Hold there, citizen. Join me in looking at the new day. Pause awhile and let us talk on the beauty of green things."

"Gladly, citizen, would I had the time. Perhaps on my way back."

So one thing leads to another. The printer insists that the man stop, but the man continues walking. The printer shouts for help, comrades rush out into the street, the man is surrounded, his pockets turned out. The printer reads a letter which he has taken from the green case. It stinks of sedition and vile atti-

tudes. They want to take the suspect to the police but
he refuses to go, so they pull at him and beat him a
little. And finally he comes to Tallien. Not personally,
but his case.

The man was petty nobility. By all accounts, Tallien
discovered, he'd been just fine in the beginning. There
were lots of them like him, and even some with big
titles, at the start, ready to join the Revolution, all
ready to put their shoulder to the wheel for the common good. Imagine, some even called for the execution of the King. Did they (wondered Tallien) think
that would spare them from any suspicion of future
reactionary intentions?

At any event, this little-title had written a letter
(discovered in the green case) to a nobleman proscribed by the Committee of Public Safety who was
living in London and stirring up trouble for the
Revolution. Tallien had read the letter four times
carefully. Try as he might, he could not fault the
prose. It was written in an excellent French. Yes, he
would have to agree with Robespierre (who had
found the letter florid, stilted, and in its sentiments
inflammatory in the hands of the enemy) that the
consideration of the danger the letter presented was
alone the issue. But what of the man's previous history, his good service to the Revolution?

"What of it?" Robespierre demanded. "Does that
keep the Reaction from using the letter to raise funds
and armies against us? A letter from precisely a man

who was once with us only speaks for how insane we have become and demonstrates how pressing the need to undo us."

"I believe him when he says he had no intention of harming the Revolution but wanted to tell an old friend the truth of conditions here—and these are the present conditions, are they not, Robespierre? Can you deny that children are playing with toy guillotines and are chasing stray cats to execute their ears? Where is the limit to what we do in Revolution's name? Should a man be punished for an accident of birth, should he be punished for telling the truth, unflattering as it is?"

"The first answer is clearly yes; the evidence is that, for centuries, millions were punished for being born of ignoble blood. And as for the second, young Tallien, the answer is yes again; truth is relative to the teller and to the use put to it by the audience. Save your arguments for larger issues, save them for someone you really wish to save; I do not think this is the time for your untried voice to be heard."

It was chastening to talk with Robespierre. He took the sentimentality from your guts even before your first coffee. With Robespierre's advice in mind, Tallien read the letter for the fifth time:

"It is the fashion to speak badly of those of us who have remained. And for the sake of fashion they exaggerate. We had planned the destruction of the Bastille long before their cry went up for its surrender, long before the mob assailed it and took it in its vulgar fury. My God! How many there were of us at Court who had read Voltaire with profit! We knew change was inevitable and desirable, even though many in your camp scoffed and called us weaklings and calf brains. Perhaps we were a minority, yet we had a voice and our influence would have brought the day to a welcome end. I mean, we would have persuaded the King that his and our future rested in the course taken across the choppy Channel—where you have found it fit and comfortable, leaving us now as before to face the buffeting of abuse and misunderstanding—and before long we would have enjoyed life on the English model and no one's neck would have been the worse for wear. So I say to you, with all respect for our friendship, which you must not confuse with a loyalty to you born from our mutual class origin, that you and your present cause prove that you have learned nothing from the events following the taking of the Bastille, that you are as benighted now as you were then. It is the arrogance of men the likes of you which has brought about the present excesses of the ruling clique, and which has driven the populace mad with fear that you shall return with vengeful forces of the kind we see on our borders under Prussian and Austrian flags.

"Because of men such as you, we here are reviled. They draw their fingers across their throats when we cross the streets or alight from carriages. We who had

wished them well, we who had petitioned His Majesty
to halt the bread profiteers and order the granaries
opened to the hungry. Now we must bear identity
papers and suffer to show them to any citizen who requests them at his whim. Now we must report to the
Committee of Public Safety week by week and are ordered to provide inventories of our possessions and
sources of income and to make lists of our friends. They
do this to us, we who took pity on their miseries and
who spoke for them. We who faced the ire of the King
and Queen for their sake. Now they mistake us for you.
And in their rage they bully even the children of our
class. Gerald, my son (you may remember him, he
is thirteen now), and I were making our way through
a little mob milling about a bakery just the other day,
when one from among them called out, pointing to
me: 'Tell your father not to lose his head.' Gerald
crimsoned and I saw tears come to his eyes. He would
have championed me and challenged them all but for
me, who led him away. Imagine a youth his age subject to that vilification because of the august parent
they see in me. A few wrong words and the lad and I
would have been dangling from a lamppost. 'Go off,
you pampered jades,' one shouted, throwing a stone,
which hit my shoulder. And we slunk off, thankful
it ended as well as it did.

"Remember these things when you think of your
country, and what fury you have churned up with
your past and present heedlessness for all but your-

selves. And I ask that you do not insult me with further requests to encourage your cause."

Well, there it was. A cut here, a passage taken out
of context there, and the enemy would have all it
wished to use against the people—the man with the
green case had indeed left himself open for rebuke.

When the case finally came to trial, everyone
wanted the little-title's head and all voted for it, and
in the end so did Tallien.

The sentenced baker was an idiot who inadvertently
had swum into the historical net. As the noblemen's
instance proved, finer fish than he would get netted.
The lesson, Tallien insisted to his mirror, was that,
since one had to allow for a dimension of error in all
enterprises, why not then in the matter of a revolution.
Better that a few innocent wriggle in the seine than
risk the victory of counterreaction, the return of a
tired and mean world.

IV

One day, browsing through bookshops near the quay, Tallien came across a volume he had cherished as a boy. He found inscribed on the inner cover: *Ex Libris, M. de Bercy*, and beneath it the familiar crest of the Owl of Minerva flanked by the burning towers of Ilium.

A slip of paper lightly glued to the flyleaf carried the bibliographical data:

Piccolomini, A. *De la Serfa del Mondo: De le Stelle Fisse.* 18 full star maps, and a number of text woodcuts. Said to be in the library of Pico della Mirandola; text frequently cited in the writings of Brunetto Latini; 4to, modern boards. Venice: N. de Bascrini, 1548.

Jean Lambert admired anew the thick rag paper (lightly foxed, but still as pliant as he had remembered it in his childhood), the hand stitching of the spine, the wonderful filleting of the gathered leaves, and the green morocco cover, embossed with tiny silver stars. Tallien's hand shook to find again this old friend who had captivated him on rainy afternoons up there in the carpeted library, the star maps pointing their way to a world above his and the human station.

He inquired the price. The seller asked for three louis—he would not accept assignats, the currency of the Revolution—remarking that the book had come from a distinguished, indeed a notable, library. Tallien frowned and replaced the book on the counter. A young man emerged from behind a curtain. He bowed graciously to Tallien and whispered in the bookseller's ear.

"Of course, for you, Citizen Tallien, we could arrange a more comfortable price, payable at your convenience," the bookseller said. "Take whatever you wish."

"That's very polite of you, sir. But I do not have much room for books."

"Your friends find space; they have carted libraries away from me," the bookseller said matter-of-factly.

"Do take at least the star book you've asked after. A present from an admirer. Put it in your splendid case."

"On the eighth of July 1792, Tallien was the spokesman of a deputation of the section of the Place Royale which demanded from the legislative assembly the reinstatement of the mayor, Jérôme Pétion, and the procurer, P. L. Manuel, and he was one of the most active popular leaders in the attack upon the Tuileries on the tenth of August, on which day he was appointed secretary or clerk to the Revolutionary Commune of Paris. In this capacity he exhibited an almost feverish activity; he perpetually appeared at the bar of the assembly on behalf of the Commune; he announced the massacres of September in the prisons in terms of apology and praise; and he sent off the famous circular of September 3 to the provinces, recommending them to do likewise. He had several persons imprisoned in order to save them from the fury of the mob, and protected several suspects himself. At the close of the month, he resigned his post on being elected, in spite of his youth, a deputy to the Convention by the department of Seine-et-Oise, and he began his legislative career by defending the conduct of the Commune during the massacres."

I myself find no such circular of the third of September written by Tallien. I have come across one signed by Marat bearing such a date, and I am not certain, because of what followed later, that Tallien would have entirely approved of it, whether or not he would have approved of Marat's turns of phrase:

"The Commune of Paris informs its comrades in the Departments that many of the terrifying conspirators detained in its prisons have been executed by the people as a spontaneous expression of their revolutionary will. These acts of justice being deemed necessary by the people at a time of national emergency, at a time when we must not worry that traitors shall stab us in the back when our revolutionary army is engaged on the front and marching to repel our attackers. The whole of the nation must surely approve the actions of its Paris comrades: we must defend our families, our children, our Revolution."

There was much ado about these killings and many staunch revolutionaries were almost soured by the affair—or affairs, for the executions lasted a few days. So many factors enter into the sad business and so much passion has been spent in defining the motives of the assailants that, even to this time, little more than the brief recitation of events is feasible.

France was shaky after the King and his wife, Marie Antoinette, tried to escape Paris—some said to join the swelling counterrevolutionaries already massing at the borders—and were apprehended at Varennes. It was hard to ever trust Louis again after that, to believe that he had not been dissimulating all along in his liberal role of a king answerable to a parliament, the role of monarch-citizen. Who knows what he had been plotting all the while, and to be frank, if you were he, would you not have been plotting against the Revolution? If you were the guy who walked into a room and everyone took off his hat to him, if you were the one who pointed his finger and said, "Sit down, Jack," and Jack gets his ass down in that chair *tout de suite*, you wouldn't be so thrilled to have to hang around just like everyone else in a big hall and pretend to listen to a lot of hotheaded breadmakers and bricklayers preach to you about Justice and the needs of the People. The King, you know, wants to pay you back a little for having given him and his family a good scare and a hard time, and you have right under your feet all these others you've taken to the cleaners, these nobles and their followers and the soldiers from the old army whose loyalty you are not sure of and the priests who are crazed by the positive lack of tenderness shown them and the whole of the priestly world with their head man, the Pope, just dying to give you the last rites and bundle you off to the transcendental pit, you have all of this and now you've also got a war on your hands. Everyone and his uncle want to give this Revolution a good bath in a tub of acid, and you're like the guy on the block who, to his own amazement, has just yesterday beaten up the neighborhood bully and you seriously wonder if you could ever do it again or if it wasn't just a fluke that you landed a punch that flattened him. You are still walking around unsure of yourself when you see the bully with a couple of his friends waiting on the corner and eyeing you up. These guys are just dying to roll dice with your bones.

You wonder if the new friends you've picked up since you became a hero yesterday are going to back you or if they'll desert to the bully's gang and join them in kicking out your teeth and grinding your eyeglasses into sparkles for the pavement. The people were jittery even in their sleep and guys like Marat were giving them food for nightmares, picturing the terrible reprisals in store for them should the Reaction rule the roost once again. The Citizens' Army was marching against the enemy. Who was left behind to defend the Revolution? What would happen should all those traitors in prison overtake the guard and rush free in the streets, free to murder the Revolution while it slept, while you and your wife slept in the clean sheets of the new order? And what would happen if all the secret enemies of the Revolution, the ones you've been told about every day, the spies for the British, Austrians, Prussians, the thugs in the pay of the King and his family, suddenly cast off their disguises and joined the escaped traitors and blew the whole little production of the Revolution back to the feudal ages? *Merde!* The priests would be back, wearing their priest's garb in the streets and cafés just like before, and they'd have their land back too, the very land you've borrowed money from your cousin to buy after the Revolution has put it up for public sale.

Tallien was in Paris when it happened. After the first episode, he went from jail to jail to alert the wardens about the dangers of the recurrence of such unsanctioned and illegal metings-out of justice. It was unpleasant for him to enter those prisons and find women and children cowering for their lives, some lives not yet adjudicated by the revolutionary courts and thus, but for the fear of the havoc of the mob, still informed by the condition of hope. And Tallien tried to reassure the mothers especially that they and their children would be protected. No fear, the Revolution was not an ogre devouring its children, and they, at least until sentence had been decided, were still its children. But Tallien could not run from jail to jail and protect their gates from the blood-seeking crowds single-handedly. And so he ran from Danton to Marat to Saint-Just to Billaud-Varenne to his old friend the actor Collot d'Herbois, asking that they organize a defense of the prisons and that they speak to the Commune to prevent further random massacres.

But it was only the first days of September and not everyone was back from vacation. Marat was the exception, and Tallien found him, as usual, stewing in his tub. August was hot that year and the Seine steamed. If you lived on the top floor, as did Jean Lambert, the heat drove you mad and there was no place to go for relief. You think that it would cool off at two or three in the morning, so you plan to stay out late in the hot streets to escape the hotter flat, but then you'd come home in the early morning only to find that it was hotter inside than out and you beat your pillow with anger at the injustice of the thing. Tallien was beside himself. In the old days, he'd be in the cool country with his father and the whole marquis's household. Jean Lambert would be under a huge, old, shady oak reading all day, and sleeping with a light blanket at night, that's how cool it would get. Now the Seine steamed and you could soften five-day-old bread in its soupy vapors. People swore that they had actually seen the river bubble, especially around Pont-Neuf, so there was not even the Seine to go to at night to cool off. No wonder many of the Revolution who could afford to had fled Paris for a break in the country that burning month.

On the first day of the massacres, Tallien was having a light supper in a small restaurant. Well, that's to say, a place that sold olive oil and wine and that had prepared for him a plate of lard (which they claimed was whale fat) and peas. The humidity was killing, and all he wanted to do was sleep until the world came to an end. He was boring everyone with his complaints about the hot humidity. "You should have joined Citizen Danton in Deauville," Mademoiselle Molly suggested, none too respectfully. "There's a lot'a breezes there to cool off the most hottest winds from Paris." [Laughs all around.] Jean Lambert had to admit the remark was amusing, and even politically clever. But even the charm of it didn't stop him from sweating into his bowl of lard and peas, and he would have done and given a lot for it suddenly to be December.

Mademoiselle Molly was the first to say that she had heard screams. Her father followed seconds behind. Then a diner—a regular—whom Jean Lambert generally never took notice of, a certain Julian Rios, a retired Spanish sailor who, so he said, had been to the Americas and back and who had seen there Lafayette and George Washington ride side by side at the head of a revolutionary army of citizen soldiers, rose from the table, spilling his plate of peas and lard over his lap, and swore he, too, had heard screaming. All but Tallien had heard the screams. Paris was so still, how could you miss the shrieks, unless you were deaf, this Julian remarks. So Tallien really puts his ear to it, and finally he also hears the screams, coming from the direction of the prison of the Abbaye of Saint-Germain-des-Prés. Maybe it's a fire! Or maybe a cool, fresh rainstorm, and they were hearing the grateful shouts of those joyously caught in it. It would be great to run over to that quarter and solve the mystery. But with all those peas and chunks of lard in his guts, how can Jean Lambert move? It's the sailor who gets him going. "Citizen Tallien," he whispers, "let's go quick, maybe the prisoners have escaped."

By the time he was finally admitted into the courtyard, the killing was over. The corpses, some still twitching, were mounted in an incoherent pile. Men, women, teenagers of both sexes, and, from what Tallien could discern in the sooty torchlight, many priests still in their priestly robes.

"The criminals tried to escape and the people caught them," a man with a bloody saber said to Jean Lambert.

Tallien thought he saw the man wink at him. One of the others in the group laughed and pointed his pike skyward. "Now they are flown to heaven, but we got their shitty bodies right here."

"Go home, Citizen Tallien, the Revolution needs you to write another speech."

"Get some paper and put down on it that the people know how to take care of traitors," said another, the most precise-looking of the band.

"What are your names?" Tallien asked.

"My name," said one who had not yet spoken, "is Citizen Razor, and I am the one who likes to shave down the ears of bookworms. You have giant big ears, Citizen Tallien. Come here and sit on my lap and I'll trim the fat off them."

Julian tugged at Jean Lambert's sleeve. "There is nothing we can do here, citizen."

Bottles crashed about them as they reached the outer gate.

The massacres continued five days longer, and Tallien could find no one to stop them. Danton, just back from Deauville, shrugged his shoulders. "What am I to do when the people wish to express their will?"

Marat grinned. "The people can now sleep safely at

night, Citizen Tallien. Isn't that worth the death of a few who would harm them?"

The Princesse de Lamballe had served the Queen for several years. After the Revolution seemed to be getting out of hand, Lamballe and her husband, a good fellow who merely wanted his meals served on time and served hot, made off for haven in London. Hardly settled in, the Princesse had a change of heart.

She pined for her mistress and grieved for her mistress's dismal plight, stuck away, as the Queen was, in cold, stony quarters, a story or two above the King, her husband. And the more Lamballe grieved, the more guilty she felt for having deserted the Queen's side. Her husband tried to console her by pointing out that there was not much help she could offer her mistress, and that everyone understood her concern and respected her no less for having decided to wait out the evil days in the warm grace of the sympathetic, if stolid, British.

These were exactly the words least certain of creating her husband's intended effect. The Princesse sat by the bay window overlooking the benign plants of the Physic Garden and tried to send her Queen a telepathic message. But the waves were going the wrong way and she, instead of sending, began receiving impressions from the imprisoned Queen. Marie Antoinette appealed to the Princesse in a tongue alien and barking, and it was some moments later that she realized the Queen had been addressing her in her native

TALLIEN *A Brief Romance*

German dialect, a form of Austrian patois, just the
form her detractors had all along accused her of speaking when she wasn't butchering the French language
in public. Just as the Princesse thought she would go
mad with frustration—since she neither spoke nor
understood a word the Queen was uttering—the
Queen must have understood her thoughts and broke
into the more familiar, though heavily guttural,
French. In that language, she let it be known her heart
was broken.

Many were cruelly against her and sent her
recently published pamphlets giving supposed evidence of her raunchy infidelities and of her especial
love for the tall, fishy Swede, Count Axel Fersen,
with whom, it was claimed, she had invented swinish
new forms of bed-bouncing. She was despised and
reviled and friendless. Yet, and on this point the
Queen was adamant, those of her friends who had
found safety were to remain in their places of security.
She sent the Princesse her love and wished her happiness.

That settled it. Lamballe rose from her communica-
tion and announced to her husband that she was
returning to Paris to stay by the Queen in her agony.
And despite pleas and the like from husband and fellow exiles, she sailed off for Paris, where she was soon
arrested and imprisoned as a traitor who had joined
the British service and who had come home to sow
discontent. That the Queen knew of the return of the

well-intentioned one is unlikely, kept, as she was, apart from all encouraging information and favorable turns of events. It is more than likely, then, that when on the second night of the massacres a mob took the Princesse de Lamballe, along with some fifteen other women and children, out from their common cell and into the prison courtyard, and demanded she abjure the Queen and say that the Austrian was a whore who had spread her legs for half the army of Prussia as well as for the whole sex-crazed court of Versailles, and when the Princesse refused to comply, proclaiming instead that they were ignorant of the sweetness and virtue of their Queen, a man in a red bonnet stuck his pike into her and others broke and twisted and hacked the arms and legs from her body and another opened her chest and ripped out her heart and another cut off her breasts and impaled them on pikes, and the man who had taken her heart later roasted and ate it, and her breasts and her sex and her head were later paraded through the streets, the Queen knew nothing of these events until they were reported to her in fulsome detail the following morning.

Rumors suggested that the massacres were not a spontaneous expression of popular fear and rage but the contrivances of Marat and Danton, and that the Citizen Revengers in reality were thugs and assassins, themselves released from prisons and in the pay of the Commune. But no one would confirm this rumor, and Danton, when pressed by Tallien, dryly noted that calumny against the Revolution takes many forms, this rumor being one, and that Tallien would do well to remind himself that a huge counterrevolutionary army led by the Duke of Brunswick was less than two hundred miles from the walls of Paris, and while what had happened to the Lamballe woman was not a result of instituted policy of the Republic, the invading army, almost at the door, officially had announced the most monstrous reprisals against the Revolution and its upholders, the ordinary people of France.

All the same, Tallien begged, could not the Commune proclaim its disgust at the illegality of the attacks, could it not disassociate itself from the gauche fury of the mob, while maintaining its promise of legal pursuit of the counterrevolutionaries. Of course, that could and would be done, Danton assured him. Yet, on the third day of the massacres, the Commune issued Marat's letter calling for support of the massacres throughout France.

On the fifth, and, as it turned out, last day of the massacres, Tallien was beside himself. No one even pretended to pay the least bit of attention to his protests and his pleas, and it was clear that he was becoming a nuisance. After all, who wants an alarmist sadsack around, a worrywart giving everyone the itches. Tallien read the dark signs and considered taking a long trip to America until his friends had forgotten what a pain he'd been and began to remember him again in glowing terms. Instead, Jean Lambert took to his room and to his bed.

In those days, if you had to get an important message to someone, you had to send a messenger. But, even in those days, few persons sent messages at three-thirty in the morning. Imagine, then, Jean Lambert's chagrin when he was shot out of his world of dreams by the pounding at the door. What couldn't wait until eight or nine in the morning? In revolutionary times— and this is one of its attractions—people tend to stay up late, they hang out and talk and sometimes make plans through the day and night. Who wants to go to sleep when there is so much excitement? And when the weather is warm, as it then was, the Revolution is like a block party. Each hour is so fervently packed that you can't imagine how you had ever loved your dull, pre-revolutionary life or how you could ever return to it. In the clubs and in the cafés, revolutionaries of every political color made their deals and hatched their partisan plots, regardless of the hour.

In the club room where Danton sat, things could have looked better. He was in a funk. He was getting *beaucoup* heat for the killings in the prisons. Even guys in his own faction were pounding his ribs for making them look bad. He had to take action quickly, but it would not be the best move in town were he to come to his own defense without there having been, as of yet, any direct accusations made against him for the murders. Too much apparent self-interest stinks even in the most venal circles, so imagine what a farce Danton's opponents would make of his protests of innocence in the business of the prison bloodbaths.

At about 3 in the a.m., he hit on a thrifty solution and took quill to paper and, in a short while, had composed a note and seen it dispatched.

At the pounding on the door, Jean Lambert thought he had made such a creep of himself to the Commune that they had decided his turn under the People's Blade of Justice had come, and he hated himself for not having heeded Julian's advice to beat it to the sheltering oaks of the sapling Republic. It was some of this self-hate that made him think of diving out the window head-first and giving his brains to the pavement, and, with this shortcut leap to oblivion, saving himself and the People's Tribunal several wearisome hours of judicial theatrics. But the image of his creamy brains steaming on the morning pavement was so disgusting that he rushed to the door as if it were his salvation and opened it without inquiring who was so impatiently waiting there.

It was, of course, the messenger sent by Danton. In those sincere times, no one expected to be tipped, and Tallien offered none. [Exit the messenger.]

The note had its merits. Tallien, it explained, was to have a say in the supervision of the prisons and in the future roundups of the subversives and conspirators, and he was to be given the chance to explain the ideological design and legal grounds of such prosecutions and arrests. In his forthcoming address to the Convention, however, Citizen Tallien would do well to point out that what had passed had passed, and that no one's interest would be served by raking up the gory story of the Lamballe woman, or of any other unfortunate detainee, for that matter. The point, Danton emphasized, was to look ahead, not backwards, and to get on with the noble design of the Revolution.

Jean Lambert rushed to the window, not to sail out of it, but to call down the street. Incredible as it may seem, the messenger was just turning the corner. Tallien's attic was so high and the messenger so slow of foot that even though it had taken a full five minutes for Tallien to read the note, make a decision, and start to frame a reply, the man had not even gotten to the end of the road. By the time he had remounted the stair, Jean Lambert was penning into the first paragraph of his address.

The heat wave had passed, and tempers with it. In the cool and fresh morning, the sun filtered through the windows with remarkable subtlety so as to suggest, rather than to declare, itself present. The Convention assembled with renewed interest of purpose, and doubly so, now that a virgin speaker, Jean Lambert Tallien—authentically of the people and a self-declared regicide well before the mass leap on the king-killing bandwagon—was to make his maiden address. Heretofore he had belonged to no party and to no faction, and so, elevated on the platform of disinterestedness and with the fillip of his youth, he was greeted warmly by the Assembly as he approached the dais.

Tallien mounted, his slender body erect, and brushed aside the black curls furled about his forehead. He withdrew some pages from his green portfolio, and he studied them for a few moments before going on to speak without further reference to them.

He commenced:

"Citizens, children of the Revolution, my nature is no higher than yours, citizen brothers, citizen sisters. For Nature needs instruction from models higher than itself, from natures pure, incorruptible, bound only to Reason, swayed only by Reason, in love only with Reason. Thus should my brothers say: Halt this excess, stanch the blood flow, return us to peace; if they should say: Return us to Chardin, Boucher, Fragonard; give us serene, unbloodied landscapes, a maid and milk cow in the foreground, leafy trees and gentle hills in the background; if they should cry: In the name of heaven! Give us a restful night in bed! Where, then, should I find in my brothers the higher Nature which I long to follow?

"Nowhere! And then I, too, may say with my wayward brothers: Open the dungeons, usher out and escort the nobles into the light of the Paris day. Let us share our bread with them—as they did with us when we cried out frozen and hungry under their brilliant windows; give them our seats, here in the Assembly, as they did theirs in their wide halls and warm parlors when we begged to be heard, so we may discourse and learn from them the way to Justice. Let us beg their pardon and, like penitent children, implore their love. Yes, summon our best tailors to sew, with their finest stitches, necks back onto wronged bodies, and let our revolutionary breath inspire their corpses back to daily life. And all will be sweet again, as before." [Shouts: "No! no! Forward the Revolution! Forward the Commune of Paris!"]

It was soon after this speech that Tallien cast his lot with the Jacobins, and was warmly received by them. Marat was particularly pleased and sent Jean Lambert little notes hinting that he wished to take the youth under his scabby wing. But these overtures came to little. Jean Lambert was too nervous in the invalid's presence for any alliance to be forged. Marat gave him the willies with his fricatives and acidic hiss.

"Swindlers, villains, thieves, secret agents, double agents, and triple agents, gutter rats all of them. They preach revolution, but they practice dissolution of all our gains and they would bring back the monarchy and invite the Austrians and the British to squat on our heads. We must stop them, young Jean Lambert. We must skewer their gizzards with the people's bayonet. Now, this instant, before it is too late. And if I need to remain in this tub, it is you who will be my voice and my arm."

It was not against the nobles Marat was saying this but against fellow revolutionaries, the Girondists, and even against those of Marat's own faction, against Danton and those virtue-filled worthies Robespierre

and Saint-Just. There were plots, cabals, and con-
spiracies everywhere except in Marat's tub. But Jean
Lambert and he would fix things up for good, and all
it would take was a few hundred selected heads. Five
thousand at the most. When Jean Lambert left Marat,
he felt itchy and feared his skin had caught the sick
man's affliction.

Jean Lambert wished Danton had been as solicitous
of him as had the tub man, but Danton spared time for
no one but his old drinking friends and his young
bride. And Robespierre, who Tallien felt had much to
teach him in the way of precision of bearing and in
the daring of his crushing rhetoric, was closed to
everyone but his brother and Saint-Just. As for others,
each went his own way, or they went to their families
and lovers. And Jean Lambert, even with his minor
luster, had to eat his meals alone, and not in glamorous
restaurants where the owner or the maître d' knows
you and invites you for a drink at the bar and intro-
duces you to a few good-lookers and their swell pals,
so that after a few drinks everyone is feeling friendly
and you start to talk about this and that and even a
little bit of the other, and then, at a certain moment,
someone says, Citizen, join us for dinner, and you
play hard to get for a few seconds, and then you say,
Hey! I guess my friends got caught up at a feast of
Reason or a banquet of Justice and have forgot all
about our *rendez-vous*—or is it *rends-toi?*—[laughs
all around] so why not, sure, I'll join you for a little

something. Soon you are all on a first-name basis and
you hit it off with everyone, especially with little
Miss Marie Roget, who, thank your lucky stars, is not
with the guy she came with but is only his old friend,
which leaves you free to make a few moves toward
her avenue. Then, as you are all leaving, you say,
with special looks toward Marie, "I have my carriage waiting, can I drop someone off somewhere?"
and then, in the jostle of goodbyes, you lower your
voice and you say, "Marie, when can I see you again?"
And she says innocently, "Why, I'm always around,
you can see me anywhere." You frown a bit so that
she'll know you're not kidding and you mean it, and
you say, "You know, I mean, *see* you for a dinner, or
a pony ride in the Bois or a picnic on the Île de la
Grande Jatte (of course, she can take her cousin, and
you'll bring a friend along, too—maybe Marat will
be able to step out of his tub for a few hours), or you
can take in a play or an opera. She smiles and says,
"Well, maybe," although she doesn't know where a
man as important as you can find the time to sacrifice
your work for the People just to go out with her, but
maybe, if you really want to, something could be arranged. That's how it would go if you were young
and lucky and could afford to go to fashionable spots
and you were not in the swing of social life and dinner
parties or not connected to a wife or a lover. Tallien
was not able to afford such fashionable spots, and as
he was neither rich nor powerful, he was not sought

after by society. How did young people meet one another in the eighteenth century? Families arranged most marriages, and Tallien was off the family circuit. Boys and girls were not sent off to coeducational schools where they could flirt in classrooms and make library dates. You couldn't just go to a movie on Saturday afternoon and hang out around the candy counter with your friends and sort of make eye contact with someone you'd like to take up to the balcony and try to feel up. Girls, unless they were streetwalkers, just didn't parade around the streets meeting guys. There was no way in those days you could take a stroll in the Luxembourg Gardens and spy a lovely one reading alone on a bench and sit beside her and say, "*Candide*! I've read that. Delightful book, is it not?" and by that maneuver strike up a conversation which you might carry over to a café and then to anything else you two may later care for. Jean Lambert Tallien wasn't the pickup type, in any case. A certain verve is needed for that, and not the kind usually possessed by bookish people.

Seeing him get lonelier by the hour, a good friend would have fixed him up and they could double-date, take in a play and a little light supper after. Danton's ravishing teenage wife, Anabel, knew a salon full of good-looking girls her age (with personality!) who would have been crazy for a handsome and sensitive guy (and a good talker) just a few years their senior. But Danton was so passionate for his bride and so frightened that someone exactly fitting Jean Lambert's description would come along and take the sexy little wife away that he never introduced her to anyone unless the citizen was approaching senility. Thus, you could forget the whole fix-up theory.

In short, Jean Lambert stayed in his attic a lot, pains of sadness foaming in his throat like an invasion of burning pus. After all, how many books could Tallien read, how many speeches could he write, how many prisons could he inspect, how many reactionaries unmask before the longing for companionship set in?

He applied himself against loneliness as best he could, and began to read whenever he was alone—at dinner, say, or in bed, where he read himself to sleep. A published story found among the papers and effects of a captured British spy had especially captivated Jean Lambert in spite of its patently anti-revolutionary bias and its prose as shopworn as its politics. Though it was written in a stilted and portentous English— or was it a translation from some yet more pedantic tongue?—Jean Lambert, with even his limited knowledge of that language, recognized the tale as a bloodless shadow of its radical gothic archetype.

The story was about a certain Gottfried Wolfgang, a young German student, an Idealist, whose brains were packed with passages from books dealing in transcendental truths and spiritual essences. He studied these books night and day, until his shoes no longer touched the pavement and his head bumped the puz-

zled clouds. Gloomy he became, and, to his friends
and family, more than a little strange. For his health's
sake it was decided that he should change his geog-
raphy, and therefore Gottfried was sent to Paris,
where, it was hoped, the attractive lights of the city
might lure his mind back down to thoughts of the
human street. But let the story, somewhat modified,
tell itself:

Wolfgang arrived in Paris at the breaking out of the
Revolution. The popular delirium at first caught his en-
thusiastic mind . . . but the scenes of blood which followed
shocked his sensitive nature, disgusted him with society
and the world.

Wolfgang, though solitary and recluse, was of an
ardent temperament. He was too shy and too ignorant
of the world to make any advances to the fair, but he
was a passionate admirer of female beauty, and in his
lonely chamber would often lose himself in reveries of
forms and faces which he had seen, and his fancy would
deck out images of loveliness far surpassing the reality.

While his mind was in this excited and sublimated
state, a dream produced an extraordinary effect upon
him. It was of a female face of transcendent beauty . . .
It haunted his thoughts by day, his slumbers by night;
in fine, he became passionately enamored of this shadow
of a dream.

He was returning home late one stormy night, through
some of the old and gloomy streets. The loud claps of
thunder rattled among the high houses . . . He came to
the Place de Grève, the square where public executions

were performed. The lightning quivered about the pinnacles of the ancient Hôtel de Ville and shed flickering gleams over the open space in front. As Wolfgang was crossing the square, he shrank back with horror at finding himself close by the guillotine.

Wolfgang's heart sickened within him, and he was turning from the horrible Engine, when he beheld a shadowy form, cowering, as it were, at the steps which led up to the scaffold. A succession of vivid flashes of lightning revealed it more distinctly. It was a female figure dressed in black. She was seated on one of the lower steps of the scaffold, leaning forward, her face hidden in her lap, and her long, disheveled tresses hanging to the ground. He approached, and addressed her in accents of sympathy. She raised her head and gazed wildly at him. What was his astonishment at beholding, by the bright glare of the lightning, the very face which had haunted him in his dreams. It was pale and disconsolate, but ravishingly beautiful.

Trembling with violent and conflicting emotions, Wolfgang again approached her. He spoke of her being exposed at such an hour of the night, and to the fury of the impending storm, and he offered to conduct her to the arms of her friends. She pointed to the guillotine— its raised blade glistening in the flashes of light—with a gesture of dreadful signification.

"I have no friend on earth!" said she.

"But you have a home," said Wolfgang.

"Yes—in the grave!"

An electric giddiness seemed to lift him from the ground. "If my life could be of service, it is at your disposal."

There was an earnestness in the young man's manner that had its effect. The simplicity and honesty of his dress and the foreignness of his accent, too, were in his favor . . . and within moments, the homeless stranger confided herself implicitly to Wolfgang's protection.

On entering his apartment, the student, for the first time, blushed at the scantiness and meanness of his dwelling. He had but one chamber—an old-fashioned parlor, heavily carved, and fantastically furnished with the remains of former magnificence, for it was one of those hotels in the quarter of the Luxembourg Palace which had once belonged to the nobility.

When the lights were brought, Wolfgang was more than ever intoxicated by her beauty. Her face was pale, but of a dazzling fairness, set off by a profusion of raven hair that hung clustering about it. Her eyes were large and brilliant, with a singular expression approaching almost wildness.

In the infatuation of the moment, Wolfgang avowed his passion for her. He told her the story of his mysterious dream, and how she had possessed his heart before he had even seen her. She was strangely affected by his recital, and acknowledged to have felt an impulse toward him equally unaccountable.

It was the time for wild theory and wild actions. Old prejudices and superstitions were done away with; everything was under the sway of the Goddess of Reason. Among other rubbish of the Old Time, the forms and ceremonies of marriage began to be considered superfluous bonds for honorable minds. Social compacts were in vogue. Wolfgang was too much a theorist not to be tainted by the liberal doctrines of the day.

"Why should we separate?" said he. "Our hearts are united; in the eye of reason and honor, we are as one. What need of sordid, man-made forms to band high souls together? Let me be everything to you, or, rather, let us be everything to one another. I pledge myself to you forever."

"Forever?" asked the stranger solemnly.

"Forever!" repeated Wolfgang.

The stranger clasped the hand extended to her: "Then I am yours," she murmured, and sank to his bosom.

The next morning the student left his bride sleeping and went forth at an early hour to seek more spacious apartments suitable to the change in his situation. When he returned, he found the stranger lying with her head hanging over the bed, one arm thrown over it . . . When he took her hand, it was cold—there was no pulsation; her face was pallid and ghastly. In a word, she was a corpse.

The police were summoned. As the officer of police entered the room, he started back on beholding the corpse.

"Great heaven!" cried he. "How did this woman come here?"

"Do you know anything about her?" asked Wolfgang anxiously.

"Do I?" exclaimed the officer. "She was guillotined yesterday."

The officer stepped forward, undid the black collar around the neck of the corpse, and the head rolled to the floor!

The student burst into a frenzy. They tried to soothe him, but in vain. He was possessed with the frightful belief that an evil spirit had reanimated the dead body to ensnare him. He went distrait, and died in a madhouse.

———————

This tale seemed to belong to another time. Its emotional weight was balanced toward beliefs now stuck away in the warehouse of the Old Regime with its spiritual armchairs and metaphysical beds. Prophetic dreams and intimations of love—nothing more than the secondhand trade of outmoded, romantic literary conventions; and Tallien and his generation would one day rid the world of everything that had engendered them, along with the rest of the reactionary dust and spools of old tinsel. It was the vigor of love that the Revolution would bring, and the union of whole humans, not the spellbound conjunctions of phantoms.

Still, for all its transmaterial razzle-dazzle, Jean Lambert had to admit the tale spoke to him. To roam the streets at night and come upon a beautiful young woman of the people, to fly in the face of all social restraints and pointless inhibitions and join together till dawn takes you each away—was that not a story the Revolution might one day limn into its fresh pages? In such a way did Jean Lambert spend his free hours reading and thinking. But this is not to say that he spent all his spare time in such a manner.

They were, after all, breathtaking days, and Jean Lambert was no tame youth stuck in a seminary who looked up longingly from his studies and out of his barred window to count heaven's sparrows on the wing. Once he traveled as far as the Bois de Boulogne and lunched on a porridge made of goose liver and fish roe and walked back home in the orange rays of cold light. Winter had again set in and the streets were empty. Still, there was human fire in the icy air. The

Revolution, of course, wasn't just waiting around for spring in order to march to its future. It was on that first of those implacable, freezing Februaries (the twenty-sixth of Ventôse, to be exact) that were to follow until well after Napoleon Bonaparte had left office that Jean Lambert Tallien and the Convention voted for the execution of the King.

France was at war with Austria. King Louis had voted for that war and had spoken publicly for the victory of the revolutionary army. But, one day, documents were discovered in the hollow leg of a desk in the monarch's bedroom proving that Louis had been playing a double game and had provided the Austrians cause to believe he was secretly in support of them. Even those who had given him the benefit of the doubt when he had been apprehended fleeing at Varennes could no longer deny the current evidence of the King's deliberate treason. The time had come when the King's pickle was beside the legal point. Except for those who hated him personally, it was not Louis, the wispy guy who was just hanging on to his lower lip and trying not to bawl in public, whom the Convention wanted killed, but they did not know how to tumble Louis's crown without chopping off the head on which it was, in much of the world's eyes, rightly fastened. Jean Lambert pitied Louis's person, and so did anyone and his uncle who had a grain of feeling. But after all the placards ("The King feeds his carps," etc.) and the arguments and justifications he had put forward from the earliest moment of the Revolution, what was Jean Lambert to say now? That to ask for the King's death when it seemed impossible to effect it was one thing—the noise of youth—but to vote for it when it was a likely reality, when you could see the deadbeat's pathetic face ten feet from you, when you considered that, king or no king, Louis was just another shrimp out of Mother's basin, that was still another matter. Nonetheless, when the vote was called and Jean Lambert's turn came to answer, he felt he had to override himself or at least that self who would have wished to save even a rabid dog from drowning, and he said, "Yes, the blade." And so they expedited Louis, detaching crown from head and head from body, and tossed the salad raw without coffin or shroud into a lime-filled hole only a few knew the whereabouts of.

Elected a member of the Committee of General Security, Jean Lambert moved up a notch on the revolutionary ladder. His vigor in the prosecution of enemies of the Revolution earned him the trust of all factions and persons and he was sent to establish the Terror, organized by Robespierre and the Committee of Public Safety, throughout France.

It was on such a mission to Bordeaux that he met, while she awaited execution, a young Spanish woman, Thérèse de Fontenay, née Cabarrus, the widow of le Comte de Fontenay, who had recently gone under the blade.

In a play performed three nights on the London

stage years after these events took place and written by the actor-playwright revolutionary Jean-Marie Collot d'Herbois during the final months of his life spent in hellish exile in Cayenne, the imagined initial encounter between Jean Lambert Tallien and Thérèse de Fontenay opens Act One.

Raise curtain. Scene: a cell large enough to hold a small lion. A cot; two wooden chairs; straw and mattress stuffing scattered over the otherwise bare stone floor. The cell is illuminated by a single lantern. A woman, THÉRÈSE, stands pressed to the cell bars, her arms clasped behind her. A man, JEAN LAMBERT TALLIEN, stands outside the cell.

JLT: In the dimness of this room, madame, you radiate. A glittering, serene star, even in this dusky atmosphere.

TDF: A dazzling and welcome greeting, citizen executioner. Oh! Forgive my error, perhaps you are just the cart man come to convey me to oblivion.

JLT: Neither, my dear woman. Your friend.

TDF: Is the blade my friend, then?

JLT: Not the blade, my bosom.

TDF: My cub, save your charm for the living, they are quicker to respond.

JLT: You are the most sentient animal in all of France. Witty, too, I should say by the measure of your costume.

TDF: Short measure, you mean.

JLT: A ravishing breast bared in the style of Mother Republic is ample measure for my feasting eyes.

TDF: Perhaps you are a suckling? [Thérèse here slips down from her left shoulder the slender band supporting the slashed shift and thereby exposes her left breast also.]

JLF: The cell grows brighter still, madame. I'm nearly blinded by the creamy whiteness of your orbs.

TDF: And if I am hanged from the lamppost, will you see the better for it?

JLF: Put up your sash and restore me to reason, I implore you. Let me think out the nature of your question sanely.

The play continues in this literary vein. Tallien could have penned his own version, but stage writing was not in his line. Nonetheless, by all the accounts of the same incident found in Tallien's letters and what few of his notebooks remain, the structure of the event is identical to Collot d'Herbois's scene. Tallien, however, never speaks of Thérèse's "creamy orbs," and his own account differs in matters of diction and imagery and phrasing.

Absent, too, in Jean Lambert's account is the smooth emotional stichomythia, the balancing of polite, witty lines bantered back and forth, Ping-Pong style. Collot d'Herbois's literary affectations were notorious in his time. Here he was up to his ankles in swamp, his hands and eyelids swollen and burning from insect bites, his skin rotting from fungus, and he's writing as if he's still in Paris, where he changed his hose three times a day and was up to his usual tricks, modifying and rewriting plays by Corneille and Racine for modern consumption. From the second Tallien laid eyes on Thérèse, he knew it was over. His stomach got queasy and he went dizzy. His body weighed like a king-sized lead bed. He wanted to curl up on the stone floor and sleep until she went away and his life went along with her. She had cut her hair into jagged tufts and the neck was smooth, prepared for the blade's cut. One breast was exposed, the contours of the other visible. Her back straight. Her head high. A smile ironic, mocking, injured. She did not speak, but looked at him directly, as if he were an exotic and unaccountable animal in a private zoo. Jean Lambert wanted to throw her to the floor and lick her neck and bite her lips. He wanted to skewer her so that his pike pierced through her body and shot out on the ground floor of heaven.

Then he was ashamed. He had polluted her with his bizarre lust. In three days she was to visit the abyss: did she need his bestial wet dream to accompany her there? Nature untamed by Reason had led him to this murky jungle trail. He saw himself fallen from rectitude, mixing the trust of his authority with the greed of his longing for her. He was vile and indelicate. A model for all that those of her class held in contempt, a monkey trained to eat with knife and fork but who, no sooner left to his natural self, would soil the parquet and caper under milady's dress.

"Is there some comfort I can justifiably provide you?" Jean Lambert asked, his eyes averted from hers.

"A mirror is not permitted here, sir."

"That would be a dangerous article in such a place."

"Would it ensnare its possessor with too much vain reflection? Is it that I would fall into the pool of my self-love and thus escape your instrument? Or would said mirror engender a dangerous self-absorption leading to solipsism, and in that condition, would I discover that you and this cell and this prison are inventions of my fancy and thus disposable at my wish?"

"You could cut and injure yourself with it."

"But I could hold it up for you to shave yourself before it. Better, I'll shave you myself, and trim you too, should you like."

Weakly, feeling the thinness of his feeble replies, feeling that nothing in the world he might say would have the wit to charm her, he surrendered: "Madame, you have already shorn me."

Marie Antoinette, formerly Queen of France (widow of Louis Capet, formerly King of France), and mother of the eight-year-old Louis-Charles Capet, the Dauphin, was up for trial. It would have been better for the record had they shot her quietly off the side of a road and thrown her over a bridge and into a swollen river. Everyone remembers Antoinette's disgraceful trial, and in some courts the whole Revolution is still under indictment for it.

Thérèse pleaded with him to intercede for the pathetic Austrian. "Do it for the sake of your revolting Revolution: let it show it enjoyed one clean day. Do it so that the stink of that woman's corpse won't glue itself to you forever and repel me forever. Do it because you were a son of a woman once. Do it because I ask you."

There was less than nothing he could do, and it was all he could do to keep Thérèse herself from being carted away.

They had moved from Bordeaux, where they had dallied a week, after Tallien, in an extraordinarily effective show of highhanded double-talk and bureaucratic rank pulling, had secured Thérèse's provisional release on the pretext that he was having her transported to Paris for further interrogation involving her role in organizing the escape of proscribed aristocrats. But once in Paris, Jean Lambert moved with Thérèse into her huge apartment overlooking the Seine, there being no room for the two in his tiny attic, and the affair bloomed into an open secret. Marat would have instantly raised charges against Jean Lambert, but Marat had been assassinated and his pickled and brined heart, housed in a crystal jar in the Cordeliers Club, could no longer animate the pumps of his accusatory voice. His own life and financial conduct under scrutiny, Danton was in no position to start throwing stones. Robespierre watched and waited. For the moment, there were more important clams for his bake, and the Tallien matter could be brought up any time it suited him.

The Queen, or the ragged sparrow which passed for her, perched at the edge of a wooden chair while charwomen and carpenters, pastry makers and chimney sweeps, printers and spies and roadmenders, whores, prostitutes, mistresses of fur importers, wives of munitions makers, shoemakers, booksellers, masons, hairdressers, all of Paris watched the proceedings. Jean Lambert had left Thérèse just minutes before and his body was still damp from their merge. Even in the stink of the courtroom smelling like the disinfected Métro stations of East Berlin, the aroma of her perfumed hair clung to him and gave him wild hope.

Someone on the courtroom floor was gesticulating and shouting. It was the prosecutor for the Republic. He loved his own words and thrilled to his own voice; he was dry-humping the courtroom with his eloquence.

"He must have practiced on his mirror," Tallien whispered to Collot d'Herbois, who had been sleeping with his eyes open. Chauvinist solemnity and revolutionary self-righteousness were stupefying the rats huddled in the courtroom cellars, and what few flies remained in the cold day were killing themselves in suicide flights against windowpanes as charges against the Queen mounted. High seriousness lived every-

where, except in Tallien's heart. The claims against the
little dry sparrow were laid on too thick, Jean Lambert thought—a kilo of rancid lard spread over a
wafer. "The Austrian" had depleted France's treasury
with secret gold transfers to her homeland; she had
built joy palaces at vast expense while her people went
to sleep starving; she had given comfort to reactionary
aspirations abroad and was an enemy of Liberty at
home. Tallien winced at the last charge. He had
heard it used often against others before, but now it
seemed a dull razor, indeed. The Law of Gravity was
an antagonist of Liberty. Liberty was an assassin of
Liberty. Sleep was a vast enemy of Liberty. Banality
was everyone's foe and tyrant. What harm could she
ever do again, if ever she had done any, except to be
her own, spoiled, ninny self. Put her under toy-soldier
guard in a little greenhouse and, like the little sparrow
she had become, let her eat breadcrumbs sprinkled
with brandy when she grew chilled with the memories
of better days.

Marie Antoinette was all dried up. Her hair yellow
like straw born in prison. Her hands bony wings. Her
cunt become a nest of troubles. For now, a new charge,
not listed in the original indictment, enlivened the
proceedings, and even Jean Lambert woke to it. She,
this woman who called herself a mother, was the lowest pervert under heaven's canopy. Her affair with the
Duchesse de Polignac was only the faintest sign of the
unwholesomeness of her unnatural being. In his hand,

the people's tool, he, the appointed instrument of the nation's Justice, held proof that this *soi-disant* woman had had immoral relations with her son, exciting him with seven varieties of perversion in order to bind him to her and dominate him when one day he came to the throne. She had placed the boy in bed between herself and the King's sister, Madame Élisabeth, and they taught him how to arouse them and to pollute himself, thereby hoping to weaken his manhood and leaving them to rule and guide the future of France.

Tallien thought he saw Robespierre draw back. Not from the prurient nature of the charges—they had been commonplace slanders found each day in Hébert's newspaper, *Le Père Duchesne*, but from what Jean Lambert guessed was Robespierre's fear that the prosecutor had exceeded himself and had compromised the trial with such sensational gibberish.

What did it matter? Her two court-appointed defense lawyers were shouted down and, one following the other, were arrested for the villainy of defending so vile a client. And as a further lesson, the guard who had brought Antoinette a cup of water as she had been led back to her cell was himself thrown in prison. In the end, the court convicted her and the Engine hacked off her lanky neck.

Thérèse had made Jean Lambert a rich pot of coffee the morning after the execution. She was worried that she had pressed her demands on him too hard and that he was growing morose and gloomy. In truth, his

worries were of a different cause. Through some
bizarre reshuffling of the political deck, he had been
elected president of the Convention.

Many eyes were now on him, and his love nest with
Thérèse produced some vulgar jibes among his col-
leagues. His record was still clean, but it started to
look manhandled, as if pulled too many times from its
folder. As they were entering the Convention's meeting hall one day. Collot d'Herbois said to Jean Lambert, apropos of nothing, "Why have you not yet
flown to the British and to your fortune?"

"How remarkable that I was thinking of asking
the same of you! I understand all your plays are being
staged there; your epic of *El Cid* has been translated
into heroic couplets, I'm told."

"You have just invented that," Collot d'Herbois
answered, genuinely alarmed. "Don't you dare voice
those lies!"

"My friend," Tallien said, trying to lighten the atmosphere, "if you don't tell the truth about me, I
won't spread lies about you."

This exchange took place during the greatest period
of arrests of antirevolutionary suspects. It was all well
and good this time and he could pretend to pass it off
as a joke, but Jean Lambert took the menacing point
and he grew frightened for himself and especially for
Thérèse, who technically was still under arrest and
could be snatched back to prison at any moment.
"Some interrogation of the prisoner!" a wit of the

Convention remarked. "Young Tallien is fishing deeply for evidence with his short pole, and his investigation might go on for years." "Some will die pumping a leaky hole to save the ship of state," replied another, concerned with creating a marine metaphor to match his friend's piscatory image.

Robespierre and the Jacobins had already succeeded in destroying their chief opposition, the Girondists, and those few who had escaped the guillotine were declared outlaws and hunted down far and wide. Some of the Girondists, whose only crime was that they had not voted for the King's death or had made anti-Jacobin remarks, were captured at the Spanish border, others at their mother's home, in places like Île-aux-Moines, in Brittany, where they devoured sweet female lobsters, and in Saint-Émilion, where they had the pleasure of drinking good wine before their arrest. Two Girondist comrades, who had hidden themselves in a chestnut forest on their last pause before attempting to cross into Spain, were caught while still eating their thick blood sausage and drinking a very firm local red. Seeing themselves surrounded, the elder of the pair calmly took a final bite of the sausage and a swig of wine and while still chewing and swallowing drew out his pistol and ventilated his brains. The other rose from the rich earthen floor and made a little speech— "Please tell Robespierre and his pallid squad that their former comrade recommends them to this district"— and followed suit. The arrest team could not decide whether he had meant to compliment the forest and the region or his new abode in either heaven or hell and thus omitted his final words in their report.

After the Girondists, everyone was skating on creaking ice and had to watch out for his every sigh and whistle. By decree, the Committee of Public Safety ruled the government until foreign and domestic peace was made, and the Jacobins ruled the Committee, and Robespierre ruled them both. A renewed vigilance against a host of wrongdoings against the People was called for. Suspects included those who did not actively promote the Revolution, those who spoke maliciously against it, and those who did not wear the Tricolor.

Suspected of having abandoned his former militancy because of Thérèse, Jean Lambert wondered why the Blade had not yet fallen on his head. He was being indulged a while, but to an end that was certain.

Thérèse poured him a cup of coffee. No woman in his life had ever prepared and served him coffee. So much the richer from her hand. Her rosy aroma and creamy bare neck and the orange on the windowsill waiting for her to peel it with her silver knife, and beyond the window, the racing blue sky lapping the world: it really was a dream. What sweet thing had he done to earn it? How could he extend it beyond the moment? She smiled and thawed his fears. She smiled again and he fought to anchor himself, to keep from leaping out the window from sheer happiness.

Before he finished his second sip of Java, he leaped toward her like an epileptic toward the spreading abyss, and they were at it again, only the deep softness of the French-made mattress preventing them from bouncing ceiling high.

"If I were not so concerned about leaving my head elsewhere, I should lose it to you," Thérèse whispered, the blue quilt tenting their bodies.

"Mine is quite gone. Look! It lies there on your lap."

V

In the halls of the Convention, he barked. He barked louder and more zealously than many others who were chiefs of barking. The Angel of Death, Saint-Just, did a good bark, but it lengthened into a growl and soon became a disquisition on property and the need for an equitable distribution of confiscated émigré lands and estates among loyal patriots and revolutionary citizenry. Robespierre came over to you like a friendly dog, a labrador or a griffon, or a tender-hearted collie, and he sniffed about you and gave a snort of delight to be near you, and the following day he returned, and while you waited for him to repeat his former show of affection, he began to bark instead, and then the others would go mad and bark even louder, and away you went to the mangy kennel for rabid suspects and wormy traitors.

Tallien's bark was a beaut. Its short yelps and husky huffs denounced moderates and reactionaries and mongrels wearing the revolutionary cloth; it demanded that the politics of favoritism be put down. It sounded so loud and ferocious you wouldn't want to come within ten yards of him. (Collot d'Herbois said to Saint-Just: "The more Tallien gets red from barking, the more I am sure he has plenty to hide.") With his bark, Tallien silenced others whose fangs were showing, and no one dared to snarl at him in public or thought it wise to trail him too close to home. Robespierre also thought not to dare with Tallien too soon, and he wagged his tail and sidled up instead to his comrade Danton, to whom only days before he had sent a letter of support so adulatory in tone that Danton, against his better judgment and knowledge of the world, allowed himself to take it at face value. And then, suddenly, Robespierre barked, setting the conclave going in chorus against Danton.

Collot d'Herbois never got further than the second act in his play of Tallien's story. The stage writer died of one of those burning tropical fevers before he could finish. His constitution could not bear the heat and the mistreatment by his guards, and the insects living in his body like bugs in the white under-

side of a rotting log. Something about Jean Lambert
Tallien must have really stuck in his throat, because
he kept on writing about him until after he was so
feverish he couldn't keep his quill in his literary fist.

Scene 1 of the second act treats a moment in Tallien's life soon after Danton was dragged howling
to the kennel and when Thérèse was most assiduous in
her efforts to have Jean Lambert get her friends out
of prison so that they might flee to safety.

Curtain. A large apartment of a *hôtel particulier*
recently commandeered by the Revolution and now
the headquarters of Jean Lambert Tallien and his
mistress, Thérèse Cabarrus.

TC: Jean Lambert, this must not be. Others are allowed
to flee to England and to the Swiss, while my
friends are persecuted and brought to the Machine. Gross boors—you and your accomplices!
Banish my friends to America. There is sufficient
punishment in that, and more than sufficient, I
would say, for delicate and sensible people.

JLT: My little cabbage, why plague those forest vir-
gins with such a breed? In two years, Madame
de Chessy and her *raffiné* circle will transform
Franklin and Jefferson into frontier fops. Perfumed saddles, gilded carriages, birdcages in the
coiffures, truffles in the savage venison. I have
nothing against your friends personally, nothing
against their persons, I mean, but we cannot
afford a policy of favoritism.

TC: As you wish, murder them.

JLT: Murder? A basketful of wigs only—the trunks may go their way.

TC: Oh! How gallant your abstractions. Give me up, too, then. Better the scaffold than to suffer you and your speaking triangles, those constipated Platonists of the Revolution, of the mob riot, I mean.

JLT: Hold! Let your lips form a kiss. Give your mouth to love, not to anger. Should not your beauty triumph over reason?

[The dress undone. A clump of blue silk on the polished parquet. Cloth breeches draped on the crushed velvet canapé.]

Those morning coffees cost Jean Lambert a lot. Had he dropped over to his usual café for them, as was his habit before living with Thérèse, the same three weeks' worth would have totaled twenty francs, even with an extra few coins thrown on top for a tip. Thérèse's home-brewed mocha and creamy pleadings obtained from him the release of seventeen of her friends ready for the Blade and cost him, in certain revolutionary circles, the full value of his currency, while upgrading hers. From the point of view of their ability to harm the Revolution, the released seventeen were nonentities; from the perspective of their political alignment, they ranged from absolute monarchist to constitutional republican to political blanks. Some were nobles who had voted for the execution of the King, and some were nobles who, missing certain of the charms of the old days, had voiced at a dinner party a few anguished regrets. One, General Alexandre Beauharnais, who had paraded a spurious title of Vicomte, had charged that battles were being lost against the Austrians because of incompetent Jacobin military leadership, and he was arrested for sedition. His wife, Rose (who preferred to be called Josephine) Tascher de La Pagerie, a svelte Creole from Martinique, entertained no political ideas but had complained bitterly at her husband's arrest and had made, on several earlier occasions, lewd jokes about the relationship between Marat and Danton. Thérèse had pleaded for the husband and wife with especial passion and Tallien tried to please her, but the General's case was too hot and the soldier went off bravely, leaving behind an affecting note, which, Jean Lambert, before reading it, passed along to Rose-Josephine in her cell: "Rose, I am a soldier. I have loved battles. None has excited me as much as you. Now I am dead. Live your life."

The Terror was moving at a quick pace and many were executed that day. The proceedings themselves, however, were becoming more sedate for victim and spectator alike. Of the sixty-four dispatched that morning, two resisted passionately, and only one, a man of fifty, slobbered and screamed for his mother. Others went their way with calm, and several left the world with flair and distinction. Except that there was no contest and no sand, the executions were like bullfights, Thérèse noted on that morning's work, which she had made Jean Lambert bring her to in disguise. "The animal is killed and it shudders," she commented after the fourth blood-soaked body was bundled off the scaffold. In Madrid, where she had seen many bulls killed in the corrida, she learned at an early age, she told Jean Lambert, to think of death as a cool afternoon shadow speeding across the arena's troubled sand.

Tallien was sure the spectacle of the execution would terrify and disgust her nonetheless, and that it would push her to despair at her own vulnerability. But she said to him when they returned home and she had removed her red bonnet: "Nothing can hurt me now except the murder of my friends."

She went to bed, where Jean Lambert found her in the late afternoon eating oranges sprinkled with rose water and cutting pages of books she had long ago wished to read. He himself did not know how to idle in bed. Nor did he ever know a bed so large and full that he could lie across the width without his legs hanging in space. She was born to it. Bed was her moored vessel and she could float on it for days. Jean Lambert could find her there at any hour, and at first he thought she had removed herself from the world from fear of it or that she was lulling herself to calm after the terrors of the cell from which he had plucked her.

He soon came to understand that, even before the Revolution, she had exercised the luxurious habits of her class, and that now, barely out of prison, she had resumed them without reference to the hardships of her captivity. Tallien marveled at her resiliency and her ability to continue her life in her accustomed mode. The periodic riots and lootings, the pockets of rabble menacing the streets, the constant threat to her and her friends' lives, the upheaval of all she had known, appeared to leave her unaffected.

She complained to Tallien only once, when her housekeeper, la señora Nuñez, tainted by the revolutionary events around her, refused to serve her mistress breakfast in bed and had sardonically addressed her as Citizeness. But Thérèse weathered the rebellion, even managing, eventually, to win the woman back to her side.

"She is an aristocrat, yes, but she is ever a great lady," Señora Nuñez advised Jean Lambert one morning, as he was on his way to have coffee at his café. He felt an uneasy instant of jealousy at that declaration. Here was Thérèse, just surfaced from her cell (literally blinking her way through the street and into Tallien's carriage), reviled and in disgrace, the lowest laborer having more status than she, by virtue of the new order, and yet she continued to win admiration when she should have been despised. In periods of transition, Jean Lambert reflected, adjustments come slowly. People's worst habits are too ingrained to die off quickly. Generations would have to pass before persons were esteemed for their merit and virtue. As for now, new standards would continue to be judged by the old values and the old by the new, each contending for its place. In the region of the Vendée, for example, those who should most have loved the Revolution—the peasants irked by the Church and the rich alike—hated it and fought it bitterly in little guerrilla actions against the troops of the Republic and had offered their soil as the staging ground for the émigré armies floated over from England. The Vendée would have kept kings and bishops and have begged for the blessing of each and gladly eaten lies and wormy bread. So much for the universal allure of reason and progress!

Thérèse had given him the names of two more she had deemed imperative he save. They were nobodies from the state's point of view, and no one was laying too close a watch on them. The father was a minor noble who had lived too long in the country, on a little estate in Fromont, where he watched the hay grow. The daughter, by Thérèse's account, was a delicate beauty of wonderful intelligence. Their deaths would have been just more ordinary dust thrown against the scattering wind. Tallien signed a folio of papers requesting their transfer from one prison to another. From there on, he knew and asked nothing of the machinery by which, weeks later, they got to London. Thérèse funded their escapes from the sale of jewels and paintings, managing even to drive a hard bargain with the picture man, who, in dealing with fallen aristocrats, knew he had the whip handle and had offered her for a Boucher a price that would hardly buy a drawing by David, then currently the rage.

"Rococo is entirely *démodé*, and these examples you have, while very good, are of little value and have few buyers. I make a special price in consideration of you and your situation, citizeness."

"A price considerate of me would be one you could never afford, and a price in consideration of my situation is one which a gentleman would never need mention."

After that little exchange, they went to the bargaining like pros in a *souk*. Thérèse hauled in nearly what she needed, and she made up the difference with a sale of some books in Jean Lambert's mounting collection.

Where shall *we* find the means to vanish should we need, Jean Lambert asked himself as more and more death carts rolled to the new execution site on the Place du Trône. Old friends, old enemies, going going gone. It was beyond imagination that he was still kicking, let alone that Thérèse was allowed to run their little household with her neck intact. He went to her room to look at her. She was sleeping, it seemed, but as he was closing the door behind him, she called out for him to return. Never had he seen her face as radiant and friendly. So beautiful had she appeared in her cell that he did not imagine she was, in normal life, more beautiful yet, but the weeks of reprieve in her own apartment, and the balm of his love, he wished to think, had nourished her and given her, at that instant, a pitch of perfection found only in some rosy portraits.

"Jean Lambert, I slept awhile."

"And did you dream of me?"

"I dreamed of a friend and lover with whom I would spend my days to the last breath, our hands and thoughts joined till we gave way to parting death."

"Am I that friend?"

"Are you not that friend?"

VI

They were washing the streets and sweeping them with branches tied to a pole. In the café, the walls opened far away to the sea, as the Seine took barge and sloop far away to the ends of the world. In a woman's thighs he had found his life. That fact had marked him out more than had his extraordinary career. But the mark was as yet invisible, and for the present, only the extravagant air of the lover showed and not the sign of a person driven by love.

The coffee was powerful, a real Hercules. It drove his heart to pump like a condemned man's with just

minutes to fuck his last fuck. But then, Jean Lambert
mused, perhaps the fuck would be a slow and measured one, a kind of even-paced and almost lacka-
daisical, tipsy ride, and not the desperate, speedy rabbit
race one would imagine in that situation. How would
he do it? With Thérèse he usually came so fast,
whether he churned her cream slowly or hammered
her button like a woodpecker on fire, that it would be
hard to imagine any one particular parting style. But
he would want—a huge barge freighting a mountain
of orange sand drifted forever across the wall—the
kind that stirred him more than the greeting handshake
of death.

By the time he took his place at the especially convened meeting of the Convention, Morpheus had taken
command from Hercules and was sending Tallien's
heart and his whole vibrant apparatus for a barge
ride on the river Lethe.

Saint-Just was mounted on the dais, his cuffs showing extravagantly through his coat. Tallien abstractly
tugged at his own, ironed that very morning by Señora
Nuñez. Saint-Just fumed. How could anyone so
young as Saint-Just be so angry all the time? Two
weeks before, he urged that all children be taken
from their parents and raised by true families of the
Republic and thus, as true heirs of the Revolution, be
blighted by no shadow of the immoral past. A week
ago, Saint-Just trounced the past and all its works,
including in his sweep pastoral poetry, samples of

which he recited for the edification of the assembled. Robespierre had followed him, declaring that the Revolution must "diffuse good writing." Tallien had thought the Incorruptible had sternly glanced his way, but it was Robespierre's trick to range his stares over a room so that each caught in them felt uniquely singled out for his disapprobation and its consequent disaster. Tallien quickly rose and agreed with his predecessors, Citizens Saint-Just and Robespierre, whose writings, he might point out, would well serve as models for a virtuous, lean, Republican prose, and he went on to declaim the need for a comprehensive extirpation of useless literary forms and genres, of which he marked chiefmost for cancellation, as it was rooted in feudal life and rivaled only the fruity pastoral as a toy of a dying class, the Epic. Only days later, in the throes of lovemaking with Thérèse, did he realize that what he had said in his calculation to up the rhetorical ante and thus keep himself running ahead of even Robespierre or Saint-Just would be taken by the latter as a jibe. Because it was Saint-Just who, only two months earlier, had published and printed at his own cost his epic poem *Organt*, which he had presented to several members of the Convention as a mark of his favor, Tallien included. Thérèse, unused to anything less than Jean Lambert's hard passion, was bemused when, in the throes of their lovemaking, he shriveled. "So, it begins so soon," she said lightly. "The chill that frosts the summer love."

Could he tell her the truth and explain that it was the thought of Saint-Just and the Epic that had frozen his bird mid-flight? And that accompanying that thought had come the fear of Saint-Just's vindictive revenge on himself and his beloved.

This morning, Saint-Just's words could have spiraled above Tallien's head and disappeared into a vanishing point of perfection. Tallien would not have noticed it. Tallien was just waiting to garner the master image from Saint-Just's pronouncements, and then he would rise and second it. Was Saint-Just claiming the Seine reactionary? Good, then Tallien would rise and declare that the Seine be plowed over with earth and stones and turned into a people's roadway. Her elegant ankles were worth the Seine.

He should have been more attentive, because now Saint-Just had gone rabid, and when he took to his seat, many in the room turned their eyes to him, Tallien, and he realized he had let his mind wander too far afield—those classical allusions seeping into his consciousness perhaps were, after all, soporific, the sleepy language of a dying culture, exactly as Saint-Just had often claimed. Now Robespierre took the dais and the silence gathered about him like the calm at the edge of a trimmed sail. There were traitors among them. (Of course, thought Tallien, there have been kilos of them from the day of the start of the Revolution. But if one went by Robespierre's count, the traitors so vastly outnumbered the authentic revo-

lutionaries that by sheer weight of number they should
already have won back the Reaction.) Traitors who at
this very instant were preparing to betray the Revolution, preparing to overthrow the Committee of Public
Safety, the Communes, and the very Convention itself.
What had he and France done to have nurtured in its
heart such vipers? Some sang revolutionary songs
louder than the most loyal, and in their secret acts had
harbored and aided the escape of the enemy. No fear,
the traitors would be nipped in the pernicious bud and
duly punished: the Revolution would be saved.

Tallien waited to hear himself denounced, but
Robespierre continued to sound the alarm without as
yet pointing to the specific blaze. Never since school-
days, when the teacher had raged and threatened the
class with whipping the naked ass of each and every
one unless the bad boy who peed in the hall confessed,
had a group known such fear. Name these traitors
before the whole Convention wets its pants, Jean
Lambert wanted to say, but a deputy recently arrived
from the provinces and as yet unused to Robespierre's
tirades spoke for him.

"Name them, let us end with them now."

Robespierre was taken aback at the novelty of
someone interrupting him, and he recoiled from the
dais. It was so unusual for the Incorruptible to break
off like that that several in the meeting—Jean Lambert
among them—boldly took the moment to call out,
"Yes, name them."

"I return tomorrow with list in hand," Robespierre announced.

"No, now, now, today," rejoined a chorus who, fearing lest their names be on the list of the condemned, could not bear the suspense of a delay.

"Cowards and traitors shall learn soon enough," Robespierre answered, gathering up his papers and leaving the platform.

The assembly disbanded, some shyly, some grumbling, most terror-stricken and fearing to meet the eyes of their comrades.

All the way home, Jean Lambert walked with a map in his head. France had become a rat maze and he sought a hole from which to escape. The ports were guarded, the frontiers blocked. Every city, town, and village had its vigilance committee, and all strangers were stopped and their papers checked. Once the arrest order for him was broadcast, there would be no place to hide. If he was lucky, he'd have time to shoot a ball into his brain, and if she wanted, maybe he'd take Thérèse with him, too, since she had expressed no fondness for prolonging the rite of passage from mock trial and public humiliation to the final axing.

Thick wax globs, clotted balls of blood, sealed the doorjamb. A notice declared that the apartment and its contents were under the protection of the Committee of Public Safety. Tallien broke the seals and entered with his key. The apartment was empty in the hollow way it becomes the moment its tenant dies or when a woman has forsaken it. Not that anything was removed or unsettled, for it was exactly as it was when he walked out that morning, but the female soul of it was gone, and now the apartment was a dim rococo cave.

It was a simple ploy, no legal parades needed. Thérèse had simply been rearrested under the standing warrant. She was taken to prison while he was with the Convention listening to the wind before the storm. And tomorrow Robespierre would denounce him for having harbored Thérèse, and he would thereby show to the world that neither his friendship with Tallien nor party loyalty could sway his incorruptible path. Robespierre had turned the trick well.

For a while, Jean Lambert walked Paris with the frightened heaviness of a man about to have his gangrened hand amputated. That lonely orphan hand. It's there now and will be gone at the wrist within the hour. Hard to believe it will really happen, although you know it will. You promise yourself to do nothing and you imagine the gangrene will disappear all by itself and thus your hand and your arm will remain joined and stay friends. Yet you've been assured by the best that, should you not part with the hand, you will soon lose the arm along with it, and so you are back again trying to reconcile the loss of the hand.

Perhaps they are interested only in Thérèse and will leave me alone; after all, I have served the Revolution better than myself, and surely for this one lapse

I may be forgiven. I will say that I was possessed, that she possessed me, and perhaps I will only be deported to the Guianas. What would he do there without her? Roast alone on the lean spit of his loneliness. How preferable the icy blade and the heady fall into the chute. He thought to discover where she had been taken and to go there and say goodbye for the both of them: they had had a fair run and he was grateful for that. What lying, cool bravado! Actually, all the world had winnowed down to her, and every cell in him was contracting in grief.

As he passed the Place de la Revolution, he spied Collot d'Herbois, his red hair in his hands, sitting on the edge of the road, weeping. Jean Lambert distrusted redheads, for they were famous for being treacherous and jealous creatures. Before she died, when he was still a young boy, his mother had warned him against redheads. Her caution had confused him, because she herself had been a rust-top, with a reddish complexion and an unbecoming bright cherry nose.

"Tallien, how can you still be walking? My dread wraps about my ankles like wet chains!"

"What? You at least are safe."

"Cruel hypocrite, you know as well as Saint-Just and Robespierre who is proscribed on that list."

"Me?" replied Jean Lambert, genuinely confused. "You're in that gang, not me."

"Is that why I sit here yanking out my hair and blabbering to you?"

Evening fell on the square, as it did on Paris. The two talked with the intensity of hungry seals in a cage. At last, after much flapping and rising and lowering of voices, they embraced and scattered.

When the Convention met the following day, July 27 (9 Thermidor), Collot d'Herbois was in the president's seat and Tallien up front, close to the dais. Papers in hand, Robespierre began to mount the platform, but as the meeting had not yet been officially convened, Tallien rose to his feet and demanded that Collot d'Herbois sound the bell. He sounded it the moment Robespierre opened his mouth, and as Robespierre spoke louder to protest, Tallien turned to the assembly and shouted: "He does not wait to be called to speak but speaks to us at his call." [Murmurs of approval and faint applause.]

Saint-Just rose with an indignant twitch and began to howl, but the president's bell drowned him out. On signal, the vice president, Thuriot, called for Tallien to speak, and Jean Lambert quickly climbed the steps, stopping a few feet below Robespierre on the platform, and, in an uncharacteristic gesture, threw out his arms. "Yesterday our Cromwell threatens us, today he insults us. Tomorrow he and his lackeys will clean their boots on our corpses."

Several jumped to their feet, crying out their approval of Jean Lambert. In a trembling voice, Billaud-Varenne called for the arrest of all insulters of the Convention, and Tallien then let forth his cannonade: "Arrest those who cabal against our integrity!"

At a nod from Jean Lambert, the little provincial who the other day demanded of Robespierre that he release the names of the proscribed rose up with a group of his country fellows and, in chorus, demanded the arrest of Saint-Just.

Tallien mounted a step higher and, his arms still outstretched, called for the vote—against Robespierre's shouts of protest. The vote had hardly carried when the armed guard took Saint-Just away screaming and looking imploringly at Robespierre and the Jacobin faction seated high in the gallery. Robespierre rushed down the platform and pleaded with the moderate faction in the Plain, who heretofore had let him have his way on every issue and on every call for a new round of purges.

"This is the revenge of traitors and counterrevolutionaries," he began. But Collot d'Herbois's bell clanged so loudly, and the shouts from Tallien and his faction sent up a wall of discord so thick, that no one beyond the second row could hear the Incorruptible.

Just then, a vision of Thérèse came over Jean Lambert. She was in bed, half naked, lying on her side, her thick breasts heeling to the crisp sheet of her bed. She was reading Rousseau's *Émile* and smiling as she slowly turned the page.

"Love me, Thérèse," he was saying as he approached the bedside, a pink tulip in his hand. She looked up, surprised to see him there, and putting the book aside, she greeted him with her arms open and with the warmest smile he had ever known.

"You," she whispered, "you, only you." And then lapsing, as she often did in moments of passion, into the language of her childhood, the Spanish of Castile, with its orange flowers and blood roses, Thérèse Cabarrus recited to him a passage from the great poem of her country, the very passage where El Cid gains the fortress of his enslaved beloved and finds her in her dungeon chained to a narrow pallet by a cold stone wall, and she whispers, the moment before dying: "Enchanted sword of my enchanter, pierce my soul."

And taking Robespierre's vacant place on the platform, Tallien cried out: "In the name of Liberty, I ask for the arrest of the tyrant Robespierre."

In the stampede to oblige Tallien, the Convention voted in roaring waves for the arrest of Robespierre and his virtuous brother, Augustine, for added measure. Presently, many others of the Jacobin faction were nominated for the purge, and along with their incorruptible chief, they were torn from the hall under escort and led away, each in varying degree of surprise and shock.

On the following day, Robespierre followed his comrade Danton, who had followed Louis, the King. Someone thought it a good joke on the corpse of the Incorruptible to throw it into the same lime pit where Louis had been left to molder in secret. Saint-Just was tossed into a common ditch, his head kissing the bloody ear of a fellow who had insulted him at a dinner party that spring.

Jean Lambert Tallien was for the first time in his life on center stage, the leader of the Thermidorians, as the group who had led the revolt against Robespierre had been named after the month of the successful coup. Many awaiting execution were released from the prisons, among them Rose and her friend Thérèse, and la señora Nuñez, who had volunteered to remain by her mistress.

Thérèse returned to her apartment, and within a week began its reconstitution and refurbishing along lines more suited to her new expectations of longevity. The floors of all the twelve rooms were scraped and sanded and polished. The entire place was painted the ruddy color of the Spanish earth as seen in July on the road from Madrid to Toledo. Tallien protested that the color invited him to feel he was forever under an earthen jar. Thérèse laughed and offered to have the painters stain the walls of his small room the same shade, so he would always feel under her jar. She spent August reconstructing her battered wardrobe and accessories. Small parcels sent by clandestine routes from London and Vienna, the émigré haunts, arrived at her door. An emerald brooch once belonging to a childhood friend executed the previous year, a gift from the girl's mother in gratitude for Thérèse's role in helping the flight of proscribed aristocrats. And many other such small, valuable presents appeared in token of gratitude to Thérèse, who now was given the epithet Our Lady of the Thermidor, by those who had surmised her part in influencing Tallien to upset the political basket.

To demonstrate that, while liberal changes were being made, the government would not consider a return of the monarchy, Jean Lambert and four other regicides were given the reins of the Republic, which continued at once to extirpate the Jacobin elements and to fight the émigré armies menacing French soil. Tallien was fêted and Thérèse bloomed. By the end of the year, her salon outshone all others and Jean Lambert glowed over Thérèse's genius in dominating *tout Paris*. She would go to London one day, she said, and instruct the English how to enjoy dinner parties properly and make them wish to retire to cigars and brandy in the bracing company of intelligent women.

Jean Lambert dreamed that one day Thérèse would emerge from the shock of her closeness to death and the misery of prison and come to wish for a more settled, domestic household. He plowed her with that intent, waiting each month for the sign of his seed taking hold. In time, to Thérèse's chagrin, one such sign manifested itself.

As she believed herself pregnant, they married. Thérèse drew up the marriage contract herself. Should they separate, he would have no claim on her fortune or properties, and she none on his. Her will was yet to be drawn up, but in consideration of the terrible events she had recently witnessed, it was agreed she would postpone framing that document until some later time. Jean Lambert left Thérèse all his books and whatever fortune and property he might one day possess.

The alarm was false. Thérèse was not pregnant. Nonetheless, Jean Lambert continued to dream that one day they would have a son and that the boy would become an astronomer and discover a new planet and name it after Thérèse.

Tallien was happy in his position for so long that he did not notice younger men than he had come to the fore. Young men who had been raised under the excesses of the Terror and for whom order and stability and moderation were paramount values. The word of the moment was "moderation," and the young spoke it reverentially in the salons and in the Convention. The moderates who had survived the Terror recovered from the feeling of gratitude toward the Thermidorians and were now wishing to prevent the stain of that sanguinary episode from seeping into the laundered sheets of contemporary life, and many shared the feeling that it would be safer for them and for the Republic not to keep at its helm men who might one day return them to the excesses of former times.

Collot d'Herbois was arrested for his part in the Terror before he had turned coat, and so, too, Billaud-Varenne. (Collot d'Herbois was in the middle of writing an especially difficult scene when he was taken, and he howled and blubbered at the injustice of the interruption.) Both were deported in irons in slow, leaky ships to the Guianas, their chains removed only after they stepped half dead on that steamy land. Several spoke cautiously for Tallien's arrest, just to set the scale straight, but his role on that liberating day of Thermidor outweighed the balance and he was asked merely to resign from the Council of Five and from any role in the Convention of Deputies.

At Thérèse's urging, Jean Lambert requested a government pension and was granted none. Thérèse supported him and gave him his own room in the apartment, where he could read all day and sleep at night or whatever it was he did there when she was gone to a party with a fresh crowd of young and forceful people. She took up with Rose and her new, young husband, an impoverished Corsican general without gloves who trailed after his bride in the halls and rooms and streets they traveled. Thérèse and Rose enjoyed themselves best when the two went out *sans* husbands, for Jean Lambert had begun to grow studious and gray and did not offer much charm to the surroundings. Fortunately, General Napoleon Bonaparte saved himself from being a heavy cannon in the parlor by cantering off at the head of an army and killing rows of reactionary Austrians who stood in the way of his liberating Italy.

Actually, Jean Lambert, with so much time to spare, was writing an epistle to History and to his future son or daughter. Each day, he penned the story of the

Revolution, trying all the while to explain how and why it had ever come about. He would want his children to know how, when he was young, most people in the cities worked long hours and could be dismissed at the whim of the employer, how most people who worked had little to eat and lived on bread and rough wine, and how from the little they earned each day they had to pay more and yet more for that bread until the cost of the bread was greater than what they earned. Some had profited from the hoarding of the grain and from the ensuing rise in the price of bread, and with those profits built themselves warm houses with huge windows and bought warm, handsome clothes to adorn themselves, while those who worked to pay for their bread froze in rooms wet and chilly and went to sleep hungry and woke and went to work hungry and with sore throats. Tallien wrote of the day the hungry rose and walked from Paris to the King's palace at Versailles and begged their monarch to release the grain from the hoarders' storage because the people, his people, were starving; and the King seemed like a good fellow who had never been told how terribly his people suffered, and now that he was told, he would see to it that the hoarding would be forbidden and the price of bread would be brought within the scope of his people's wages, and thus justice would reign in his land. But nothing the King had promised came to pass, and after much suffering and more such requests, the people marched again to the palace and by force took away the King and his wicked foreign Queen to Paris to see for themselves the truth of the people's need.

No king in France had been treated by his people in such a way, and the people began to understand that they had an immense power and could do more than just beg and wait for scraps to be tossed to them from the hands of those who despised them and made them live in such stunning neglect.

This simple tale Tallien wove together with the story of those who had led the people, and those who had led them falsely in order to deceive them in ways more subtle than the people had experienced under the monarchy. As he went further and further into his history and brought it to the day of the September massacres, Tallien's authority, with its ring of the solid and true sentence, began to fall away. He thought he discovered in that episode the bloody well of all the bloodbaths which followed, and he recognized that so much of what he had assumed needed to be reevaluated even at the cost of injuring the reputations of those already canonized in the minds of the people. It would require many years of writing to meet the task justly, and he grew frightened that unless he left off immediately—however inconclusive his text—he would end by amassing pages of manuscript destined only for the mouse and the phantoms of Decay. One morning, he wrote the title of his book on a clean sheet of rag paper:

Discours sur les causes qui ont produit la Révo-lution française

and he wrote beneath it:

For Thérèse

and beneath her name he quoted a passage from Shakes-speare, whom he was only now starting to read:

CLEOPATRA: What shall we do?
ENOBARBUS: Think and die.

The former sailor, Julian Rios, published the book for him just when Tallien thought he had reached the last of his chances, because few had liked it and no one believed it would return his investment regard-less of his liking it or not. Some found the style pedes-trian, plain, homely, vulgar—simply not good French; others thought it dull, a flat tale in place of what should have been round with excitements and rich with personages the public could toast and hate. Still others demanded to know why Tallien was so diffident on matters, to put it delicately, of the heart: the public was sure to want to know whether Madame Roland had ever visited Danton in his private rooms and whether the Queen indeed had taken her son's man-hood. A bookseller-publisher whom Jean Lambert had known as the printer of the speeches delivered at the

Convention before the fall of Robespierre came close to making Jean Lambert lose heart. "I would publish this gladly and I would bear the responsibility of the losses because I will always make up for them on another venture, Monsieur Tallien [few said "Citizen" any longer, as it seemed an affectation of an anarchic era], but I find the narrative ingenuous and the point of view vague and disjointed. Readers today expect and deserve sound goods and do not wish to feel cheated; there are so many authors, you know, who will gladly give them what they deserve."

He was about to ask Thérèse to lend him the money to print the book himself, but he was saved from that need when Rios appeared. "It is good," pronounced Rios. "A bit reserved and at times eccentric, but its design is attractive and there are some remarkable descriptive passages and several effective images." The understatement was hardly encouraging, and Jean Lambert was astonished that Rios would support the book on such flimsy grounds.

"I have had many lives, Citizen Tallien, and it would be fine to know that one of them had room for modesty. Exaggeration is a species of death, citizen, so, as I wish to live, I shall say of your book the truth: that, though you do not soar, you do not wade in a ditch of lies."

That was comforting! Jean Lambert wanted to laugh at the Spaniard and tell him to keep his money and spare the world some printing paper, but it soon grew clear that Rios had meant nothing malicious by what he had said and that he was genuinely eager to see the book in print.

Weeks after Tallien's *Discours* was issued, the journals and the press sliced the book into mulch. The remnant of the Jacobin party denounced Tallien as a floorboard viper, his *Discours* the document of a hired British agent; the émigré and monarchical factions hailed it as a testament of evil and regicidal madness; embarrassed, the moderates studied the text for its imbalances and spent pages attempting to argue against Tallien's claims that they had once been as spineless to capitulate to Robespierre as they presently were vigorously coward in persecuting his followers once the Incorruptible's power had been broken.

Everyone spoke of the *Discours* as if they had read it, but for all the controversy, the book did not sell. Jean Lambert offered to share the losses, one day, should he ever have the money. Rios appreciatively demurred and pulled out of the publishing profession and sailed (his brows singed by creditors' notes), penniless, for a new start in America.

Thérèse went to her room and read the book in one sitting. Jean Lambert waited the entire day for her to comment, intruding himself several times before her as if by accident. Finally, he could stand it no longer and, at dinner, meekly solicited her opinion.

"Certain lines are sublime and worth the cost of the book," she said. "But the Olympian view of our recent history casts shadows where illumination is needed, and it is possible that you have no light to shed, being as you were at all times at once in the center and at the rear edge of matters. Thus, while I say Olympian, I might also say you have a mouse's view, peeping, as it were, at the world from a hole in the floorboard. Yet, on the whole, your *Discours* is a worthy work, Jean Lambert. Measured against the shoddy and self-serving productions of the world today, it bears a certain dignity, and for that I am relieved and grateful, especially since I have never known that one of your strata could write in such an elevated manner."

"Life counters us at every turn, madame. I longed for a warm word and find instead an exegesis on the academic model."

"I regret your disappointment, Jean Lambert," Thérèse replied, with no further mollifying word or sign.

Dinner continued. Thérèse's dispiriting words sat on Jean Lambert's plate. If he could no longer hope to earn his way from writing, at least he could win admiration from the woman he adored. But his book had won him not even that. Instead, she had framed him as a curiosity of his class, a monkey with special and amusing talents, but none that would gain him lasting fame.

He had been without employment for many months and his bid for independence had brought him only further isolation from those in power, and he had created new enemies and revived old animosities. He could not continue as Thérèse's dependent forever, especially now that he had failed to capture her imagination. He could join Rios in America and learn to chop trees and eat wild red corn and wear huge skins against the snowy cold, but he could not imagine Thérèse joining him there and stepping among bushes and flooded paths. Dinner continued, until it was finally over. Thérèse politely kissed him good night and shut herself in her room. Jean Lambert reckoned that six more dinners like that and he would sign on as a hand for Philadelphia, where the inhabitants, it was said, knew how to read and had even established a printing press.

In the end, he was saved from emigration. Thérèse had used her friendship with Josephine, whose husband, General Bonaparte, had risen high in the army of the Directory, to enlist her help in finding Tallien a place, however obscure, in the new regime, and before two dinner parties had passed, Jean Lambert was again returned to the world.

VII

Tallien stepped off the felucca and onto the sandy slip, the color of sacked red gold from Peru. Come to escort him, his guide, in yellow galabia and pointed yellow slippers, blazed like a golden silhouette against the muted shroud of Tallien's gray cloth. They crossed the Medina, where tethered slaves, white and black, traded actively. Green and purple olives glistened in huge terra-cotta vats the colors of Aix-en-Provence; women glided by, the ends of their veil in the corner of their mouth like a mouse tail at the edge of a cat's smile. Tallien felt the heat of life rekindled in him even as freighted donkeys knocked him about, the lather of their heavy sweat frothing his breeches.

Bonaparte's door was shut to him. Colonel Zulawski, whom Tallien had known from the time of the taking of the Tuileries, told him of the General's rage against Josephine, of whom even here in the uncommon far-awayness of the Pyramids and the sleepy oasis and the unpaved streets of Cairo he had heard stories of her infidelity and her lewd escapades, of her dancing in a translucent dress, the cut of her décolleté below the line of her nipples, she and her friends, among them the Lady of Thermidor, Thérèse Tallien, née Teresa Cabarrus, dancing for the old pig Barras, Queen of the Directory, his lips sucking sherbets and lapping the pink nipples of peasant boys from Saint-Germain-en-Laye. Now the General's cup was topped with anger with anyone in his wife's circle, and even Jean Lambert, innocent though he was, would have to suffer the bitter spillage of the overflow. Zulawski was sorry to have to relate these unpleasant things, but it was better that Jean Lambert know the real motives for the General's coolness and not mistake it for some political *faux pas* on Tallien's part or some idea that the General had taken an irrational dislike of him.

Jean Lambert was twice wounded. The story of his wife's conduct was clearly incredible (the dancing part of the episode especially so, since it was not in Thérèse's nature to exert herself lewdly in order to be seductive), but he could admit some truth to it, and the fact of the admission ripped him like a serrated blade—he actually put his hand to his coat, as if feeling the ripping in his chest. And Bonaparte's rejection of him so early in the new venture boded disaster for the rest of Jean Lambert's sojourn.

"Are you feeling ill, Citizen Tallien?"

"This place sets the heart doing somersaults. I expect Ali Baba and Aladdin with his magic lamp to turn the corner."

"The magic here, dear Tallien, is to stay wholesome and not go blind and deaf, as have a share of our men."

Jean Lambert was quartered in a room above a carpet shop, while others brought to Egypt by the General as members of the Scientific and Artistic Commission, and the Institute of Egypt, were given breezy apartments and cool gardens in the appropriated palaces of rebel princes.

From his window, Tallien could see the wide Nile. It had once buoyed Cleopatra and her lascivious barge, and now it played the donkey for hides from Morocco and for a chained cargo of human souls from Timbuktu. Below him in the dusty square, caravans passed with ivory from the interior, and packs of insane dogs roamed wild—though fewer each passing day, since the General had ordered them poisoned, as they were a menace to traffic and the common good. All the wonders of the world lay beneath his window, yet in his room waited wonders just as great.

Articles written by members of the Institute for the journal he was brought to Egypt to edit, *La Décade Egyptienne*, were piled on Tallien's table. An essay by Geoffroy Saint-Hilaire on the varieties of

Nile fishes and birds; another by the famous chemist Descotils, on a scheme to make beer without hops; another on the ventilation of tents deployed in the desert; yet another on the improvement of agricultural methods to be utilized by a not-too-far-distant future colony of French citizens. Tallien was to write on the rhetoric of the Koran, and for that purpose was studying Arabic. (He was fast becoming known to the Muslim world of Cairo as Mufti Tallien, the memorizer of the Holy Book.) Drawings and watercolors there were, too. Dominique Denon, the artist who, in his youth, had painted the lovely bare shoulders of King Louis's favorite mistress, was now sketching the wild birds and broad-leafed plants of the Nile, and Jean Resceaux, who had recorded the battle of the Pyramids so boldly as to have moved the General himself to comment on the painting's novelty ("Resceaux, am I that thick orange daub there lurking among the cannons?").

The first issue of *La Décade Egyptienne* would be a stunning compilation of the most brilliant and novel research on Egyptian topics yet assembled, and it would bring honor to an otherwise merely military excursion—the General was well aware of this, being himself the inspiration for the journal whose editorship he, J. L. Tallien, was entrusted with. His association with the journal was certain to bring him glory, much needed now that his—as well as his comrades' —revolutionary allure was dimming.

To the new generation, he was a regicidal pen-pusher, and more than once he had heard that his fame rested less on his part in the Revolution and more on the fact that someone as ravishing as Thérèse could find him a worthy object of attention. That she had married him was put off as an instance of the mad times of the Terror and of the lengths one would then go to survive it. All his life he had missed the mark, his powerlessness in the face of the power of the world leading him to second-rate ventures, to being forever the aging junior partner in a growing firm. With the success of *La Décade Egyptienne*, he might yet create a new life, one of an intellectual force to match the prowess of the militaristic youth of the new chauvinistic France. Here, in Egypt, he would make her attentive to him, excited to bandy about his name in the *parvenu* salons of Paris.

Allah had given him a second start. And why not Allah? Out there, the call to prayer sang to him. It was profound in its appeal, more mystical and beautiful than the ring of bells from the Church the Revolution had tried to but could not silence. He would go to prayer and join the faith which had superseded the faiths of Jew and Christian; he would take wives and breed little Muslims and grow fat and be loved by his clan, for who is more loved than the converted infidel, and for whom if not he is the carpet laid on the oasis floor and the dates and the dry flattened plums and the clear lemonade spread out before him.

As children imagine specters in shadows for the delight in frightening themselves, he had envisioned this little Muslim pastoral to ward off his sadness. How quickly forced hopes fade from the truth of feelings. In truth, she was in Paris sifting through cool sheets. In truth, her beauty held more power for him than all the mystery of the Pyramids; he needed her as Egypt needed its Nile to overflow and wet the spent land. In truth, she was more wonderful than the Pyramids and the Nile combined, and more magical than all the disappearing turbans of the Orient with its sherbets and flying rugs.

The thought of Thérèse spun him into a giddy darkness. Before the Revolution, he never would have dreamed of being allowed access to thighs such as hers, the luscious, tight preserve of her class. But having once poached there, he found all other terrain dull and futile, its game small change.

"*J'aime casser*," Thérèse once, early in their passion, told him after a night of lovemaking. "I love to break before love turns stale, to break before boredom and children visit the bedchamber." He had thought little of those words then, counting them as the bravado of the enamored. Her flesh was still too warm and close ever to be gone coldly from him. And he had flattered himself, more from the inexperience of youth than from vanity or from his power in the Revolution or the attractiveness of his person, that when a woman as magnificent as Thérèse gave her-

self to love, she was a slave to her love—her magnificence in exact proportion to her incapacity for
surrender. Now he was slowly coming to understand
that, while he was still getting lonely hard-ons dreaming of her (how much more powerful and steeled his
Engine now that it could not travel to her and wished
nowhere else to travel), she had disjoined from his
full image and had kept with her his base silhouette,
which was fading from her memory with each passing
day.

She had become an indifferent catalyst of his sentiment. Autonomous and self-nourishing, it was she
who decided everything, whether to write him or not;
whether to notice when he was absentmindedly beside her and whether to suffer his absence. He had
given her all that power, and now he could not retrieve
it. If he played indifferent, she turned and said he was
posing; if he attempted to make her jealous, she pretended not to notice, or indeed did not notice. If he
tried—as once he did—to bully her into loving him
(even at the cost of her hating him), she grew distant
and looked at some riveting object beyond his ear as
if he were invisible. All tricks and strategies failed
him, all nostrums and sage love advice worthless.

Thinking the play on words would amuse her, he
wrote: "You are my Cleo-patria, more my country
than the France for which I yearn." His note fell on
deaf ears. Or she may not have received it, since the
British blockade was virtually unbreachable and even

Napoleon's most private letters were captured and published in the London newspapers. Another letter Tallien wrote when he was ill and fighting fever and dysentery and thought himself ready for the grave pits of burning lime reserved for soldiers dead from the plague:

"These may be my last lines, for it is unlikely I shall withdraw myself intact from my illness. When young, I swore myself to the Revolution, only now to find that a million have died so that we may bring the idea of a republic to mosquitoes and grinning crocodiles, so that in Paris a fat leader of the people may gain commissions on grain and munitions, and another, a gaunt razor, may lead his troops of the Revolution to cut a swath of bodies for his coarse-ci-can egoism. Before he died under the blade—I had no power to halt it— the bibliophile Chamfort said to me, 'Jean Lambert, happiness and disease: the body cannot bear too much of either.' Thérèse, you are my long disease, which this one I presently suffer may bring to a final cure."

It was insane of him to send that letter, should either Bonaparte's censors open it or should it be intercepted by the British. But he did send it, and send it with a feeling of abandon, of cutting off his nose to spite his ravaged face.

There were no repercussions, and from Thérèse no reply. He grew more ill and imagined many things. One scene repeated itself, the one where Julian, the Spanish sailor, whispered to him: "Maybe the prisoners have escaped." The little tin plate of peas and lard had fallen on Jean Lambert's lap and had remained stuck there forever. He was horrified and asked himself, "Does everyone imagine that I go about with a plate of lard and peas stuck to my lap, or do they think, especially in the dark, that I'm frozen fast with a dirty hard-on?"

Imagine Jean Lambert's surprise when one hot morning he saw Julian Rios himself parading up and down the narrow street under his window. Feverish though he was, Jean Lambert managed to call out Julian's name and to stumble down into the street to meet him, the two falling on one another, each the Friday to the other's Crusoe. They went to a café and talked for hours, Jean Lambert's eye throbbing from the strong sweet coffee he kept downing.

Rios had prospered in America. Indeed, he had grown wealthy and owned a narrow plantation in Virginia and was the employer of eighty-three black male and female souls, whom he had set free upon their purchase from the slave block. He had married a young widow—at his age!—and had adopted as his own his wife's son. In fact, Julian's precise reason for returning to Europe was to bring the young man for a short visit to Paris and from there to Switzerland, where he was to be generally educated and taught the skills of a lens maker. There was a solid life to be had in America for one with such technical expertise!

Jean Lambert was glad for his friend's good fortune;

life had brought him such ripe, well-deserved gifts. Then he began to tell his own story, and of the new avenues Egypt had presented him, and he even began to relate his strange dream of spilt peas and lard, before censoring himself and turning to the wall as if to watch the ragged march of a huge water bug. When he again turned toward Rios, he found the old man weeping and suddenly inflamed. "Little butcher, how can you forget that night when you did nothing to stop them from shitting on the bed of justice."

Jean Lambert was astonished, and for a moment thought he had merely imagined Rios's words. But the old man was pointing his finger at him accusingly. Tallien searched for a reply and was still trying to frame one when Rios took from a hatbox—Jean Lambert had not noticed it before—a large blue turban and gingerly crowned himself with it.

"These hats have powers, you know," Rios was saying, as he faded into air.

A week later, when he woke from his fever, Jean Lambert discovered that he had lost the vision in his left eye. It had left him while he slept. The attending surgeon prognosticated some vision might be restored one day but Jean Lambert should not count on it. Now the world looked like a frieze and humans like figures frozen in one. He did not complain. About him, soldiers of the Grand Army were dying off like flies in an oven and going blinder than ophthalmic bats. He had at least kept one eye, while most had lost both.

Others had little left before them but the return home and a pension that might or might not one day arrive. He still had *La Décade Egyptienne* and Thérèse and half his vision, praise Allah!

Finally, Bonaparte summoned him—Tallien anticipating that the General was to deliver him a brief speech of condolence for his lost organ. But the leader of the Egyptian campaign was himself doleful and expecting of consolations.

"Citizen Tallien," he began, "age separates us and rank divides our respective stations. You are a relic of a time which France would do well to cannonade to oblivion, and your prestige suffers from the horns that pedantically grow above your cuckold's ears. No, no, not a word, or I'll have you sent up the Nile, where the crocodiles will have your other eye. Now, on the balance side, it was your star that allowed mine to peep through the blanket of the sky, for had you not disposed of Citizen Robespierre, there would be no Directory and thus no Napoleon to be its servant. Hence, in some foolish way, you are my Adam.

"Now, let's whine about our Eves. You no doubt have had word from your illustrious wife that she is divorcing you and that she has become the mistress of the banker Ouvrard. No? No such word? Well, at least you have the privilege of learning it from your Citizen General, who seems to receive all the news of Paris except that of the Directory. To advance matters, let me add that if you think you are suffering—

and I see by your lack of composure that you are—
think, then, how much misery I endure to learn that
your wife and mine are cavorting in ribald tandem and
are beguiling a team of farts, young and old, as we
dodge the blows sent down by Allah."

Tallien, who had been standing all the while Bonaparte spoke, felt weak and, without being invited,
sat himself on a divan.

"Well," continued Bonaparte, a bit softened, "I
see your heart is not inured, and that you do have some
sympathy for your General, your leader in suffering."

Jean Lambert tried to speak, but the brine of the
tears of a thousand abandoned children—to summon
up an old Sicilian expression—welled in his throat.

"Continue in your post here as I shall in mine. Each
to his own duties and destinies, *n'est-ce pas*, citizen?
But what I have learned, and what lesson may serve
you, too, from my wife's heartlessness, is that faith has
fled and there is 'nothing left me but to become
totally selfish.' "

VIII

Many of my friends' fathers are dead now, and many of my friends are dead, too. My own father died three days after he deserted from the hospital tending him. Had he stayed there at his post, he might have lingered on a few weeks more. But he saw little use in hanging around the ward, waiting for the incredible pain to return and flower. He was going to meet his maker sooner or later, and under the present objective conditions, sooner was better. The revolution would have to take place without him, unless the dialectic heated up in the following forty-eight hours.

For the moment, it wasn't the revolution Rex craved

but cigarettes—Camels—and Chinese food. The hospital allowed neither, so with the help of a few pals, he skipped out for his last banquet. Chow mein egg foo yong won-ton soup spare ribs chop suey Coca-Cola. And sixty, eighty, a hundred, all the Camels he could smoke, ending them like minutes and seconds. Iconography of a pack of Camels: a desert and a scrawny dromedary flanked by two stunted palm trees in the foreground; a *ksar*—a little mud-brick fortress—and two Pyramids in the distance.

Claude Lorrain, the seventeenth-century landscape painter, observed that "the foreground in a picture is always unattractive and art demands that the interest of the canvas should be placed in the far distance, where lies take refuge, those dreams which blossom out of fact and are man's only love."

In the foreground of a room in a rooming house in Jersey City, New Jersey, Rex's corpse, yellowish, mummified, stiff as a laundry brick. In the background, an ashtray of dead Camels, the ashes of dead stars. In the receding lines of infinity, little white paper cartons of Chinese food and gnawed spare ribs sprinkled along an avenue leading toward a sky where hopes take refuge.

Outside the picture entirely, me, age ten, wondering where Rex finally went on the back-and-forth of his entrances and exits. One day he was going to take me to Asbury Park, New Jersey, where I had never been, and the next day, instead of the Ford and a rattling ride to the unknown and faraway, he had disappeared. "He's in the army," my mother told me, "and this time he'll be away a long time."

"Whenever I'm away, you're the little man of the house, and you take good care of Mom, now, you hear," he used to say before one of his trips. Of course I'd do that, brave little cadet, and when he'd return from this tour of duty, we'd all zip off to Asbury Park, New Jersey, and eat pink cotton candy and go for rides on the Ferris wheel, and on the downward plunge Mom would scream with fear and throw her arms around Dad's neck, and he and I'd just look at each other knowingly: Gosh! What we guys have to put up with! What a wonderful picture we'd make. The American working man and his family on holiday— another fruitful product of the partnership of Capital and Labor. Here unfurls a poster of a handsome bronzed Norseman (flanked by beaming wife and son), his sleeves rolled up, his muscles taut, one sun-tanned hand clasping the hand of a blond gentleman in a suit who holds under his arm a set of blue-prints, obviously the plans for the glassy, art-moderne, factory-size restaurant rising in the distance of the future.

There would never be an Asbury Park for us. Rex disappeared for good. In my fantasy of him, Rex was doing time in Dannemora, framed for refusing to call off a strike he had organized. One day the manager of the struck restaurant chain phoned union headquarters and invited Rex to lunch with him and a few business associates from Hackensack, New Jersey, to talk things over.

And Rex said: "Now that's a sweet thought, but I'd have to ask some of the boys here to come along, 'cause it would seem a trifle selfish, my going off to lunch alone with you fellas."

"Now, Rex, cut the crapola. You know what I mean. I think we can talk things over and get somewhere of benefit to us both."

"Well, hell, we can do that anytime over at the union hall. Why don't you boys come over and have a sandwich on us. Everyone would be mighty glad to have you all."

Rex was just giving them a hard time, breaking their balls and busting their chops with all that sugar he was stuffing up their snouts. He was asking for it, the jerk-off.

They had already tried scaring him two months earlier when the gentlemen from Hackensack had beat the crap out of him with newspapers rolled into hard clubs (that was a great trick of professional strikebreakers, because if the cops ever had the mind to search you in the street, you'd be carrying no illegal weapon, no blackjack or brass knuckles or twisting Mary, and anyway, when you were really done with crunching in the guy's jaw and jabbing him in the balls, you'd just unfold the paper and casually toss it into the trash basket on the corner), and when Rex finally got home he was a silly mess, with two broken ribs, his nose askew, and a few teeth floating in his gums.

Madelyn nursed him, swooning at the chance God had given her to have her Rex home, immobile, in her loving hands at last, and a few of his union pals came all the way up to the Bronx to pay their respects. Later, when he was a little better and able to get out of bed, they'd come over and play poker with him in the kitchen, my mother making coffee for everyone and Rex giving her a loving grab and saying: "Now, Madelyn, maybe we'll get the boys here some beer the next time." It was great times for me because he was home with us again and that meant the world.

On the night table in their bedroom: Lenin, *On the Woman Question*; Engels, *The Origin of the Family, Private Property and the State*; open packs of Camels, bottles of Royal Crown cola, pints of rye, a barrette. The room stinking glamorously of cigarette smoke, of whiskey stale in the shot glass, stinking of the burnt wicks of votive candles lit by my mother to accompany her prayers for Rex to come home safely to her.

Then they tried to buy him. One night, the doorbell rang and there was a man with a hand truck waiting to deliver four cases of rye. My father asked where it had come from, and the man answered that he was just paid to deliver the stuff. And my father said to return the liquor and to thank the ones who sent it but he had quit drinking and whoever it was that sent it should have a couple of drinks on him—to their health. When the man with the hand truck left, my mother asked: "What's the harm if you take a bottle or two, just for goodwill's sake?" and my father answered sweetly, "Madelyn, if I take one I might as well take the whole case, and if I take the case I'd take a Pontiac with a radio in it and maybe a nice holiday cabin up in the Catskills for the car to bring us to." My mother said: "Rex, I just asked," and she let it go at that, but in her heart she wanted him to let go of it all and to get out of it and find some work other than organizing small-time restaurants big on the blue-plate special (the hot turkey sandwich with milky mashed potatoes), because someone else could do it, some poor unfortunate without a family or anyone close.

And then they got so bored with dealing with Rex and his mule's temperament they framed him for packing a concealed weapon, a pistol in his overcoat pocket. When he was in the Tombs awaiting trial, a detective with a gray hat chanced by for a cell visit and hoped Rex had no hard feelings about his arrest and in fact he had word that if Rex would just go easy on a few regular guys and leave 'em alone and let 'em live, the case against Rex could be made so weak as to have it drop like a wormy wallet.

"That would be a pleasure and a comfort. But I guess those regular guys are going to have to start to pay regular wages, and as for me, well, we'll just have to wait and see who's holding what cards."

He was dealt three years and was lucky he didn't

draw seven. Did he think they were fingering a straight deck? The sap was allowed to bid his pair of kings. They had nothing to worry about, holding a canasta deck with an assortment of full houses and hosts of aces. And if the arresting detectives had wild changes of heart, say, and sang the "Internationale" on the courtroom floor and swore they had been bribed to frame the chump and it was they who had planted the piece on him, the prosecution could pull out a royal flush and nail him anyway and still give him a baby year in stir or maybe scramble his brains before he ever got released. ("Jeez, he ran like a bull right into my club and then he was so busy seeing stars that he fell out of a window that just happened to be open.")

Anyway, I tell myself that, by the time he got out of prison, Rex had become so unused to being a husband and a father that he decided to stay in that swift, unattached condition of bachelor-comrade, and with the exception of his legacy of three farewell letters to Madelyn and myself, he faded from our lives. Sometimes, with radicals, the Family of Man is the only family they feel comfortable in, finding the home-size unit too constricting for the scale of their vagabond stride.

Rex, let me tell it for you. The French Revolution taught our day no lesson. The Paris Commune of 1870, ditto. The Russian Revolution, the same in spades. The Cuban Revolution unhinged any message on the memo pad and Nicaragua seared the last synapse between history and recollection. If the planet doesn't first cinderize in the blasts of a thousand atomic suns, our greedy, mean amnesia is sure to turn the world into an East Berlin without museums.

East Rio de Janeiro, East Caracas, East Santo Domingo, East East Hampton, East of Eden. Our greed will convert reasonable humans with reasonable hopes into live ammo, and the ones who follow them will know only lunatic revenge, and the ones following them, only the post-revolutionary state parceled out among flunkies and underlings and bureauristocrats with *ci-devant* disco shades and sporting tailored polyester leisure suits designed in East Paris and hand-finished in East London. Wait and see what you will have created with your greed and deliberate, proud ignorance—post-revolutionary types who will filter your brains with the shredded pamphlets left over from the Struggle, a breed who will overhaul your genes should they think you are enjoying yourself too much or for appearing in public without a smile of social content. So what, you say. It won't happen before your time is up, and when you're out of the horny show, who gives a flying fuck who is putting the hot steel bit in whose gums. Life begins and ends with you, you say. And who can prove you wrong?

IX

Napoleon was losing Egypt, but he was more fearful of losing Josephine. You may laugh all you want, but at that juncture of his destiny he was still able to regret the loss of the latter more strongly than that of the exotic real estate he had sought to conquer. When he fled Egypt, leaving his army there to linger and die, waiting ahead for him in France was possible disgrace for having walked out on his legions, and the as dreadful prospect of divorce. Napoleon was stuffed with his wife's infidelity, with the demoralizing feeling that, while the world jumped to attention at his nod, he could not get the woman he loved to stay out of the sack with any Tom, Dick, and Henri in a tight uniform. This time she was ferrying between Barras, the boss of the Directory (and Napoleon's chief, as well), and a young stud with a brain the size of a kid's thimble, Hippolyte Charles, an officer in Napoleon's own army, who had been stationed in Paris and was wearing out half the mattresses of the classier beds of that city while his General ate sand in Egypt.

So Napoleon took off in secret, without a goodbye, like a Bedouin breaking cold camp before the first rumble of desert light, and he left his army and his Institute to work out for themselves the details of their slow extinction. Some of those he left to bleach in the adamant sun were really pissed off and you could hear their unsophisticated screams all the way across the Mediterranean as far as Palermo. Some didn't believe Napoleon had split camp and deserted them, and thought it was a story let out as a ruse, a ploy of war, to an end only he, their General, had wisely foreseen. When Jean Lambert heard the news, he knew immediately that it was true, that it had been inevitable and, from the point of view of passion, even necessary.

He was stunned, nonetheless, as if felled at the braining gate, and he understood that now he was to be off on a strange voyage. One where he would be the solitary helmsman at the wheel, the galley slave alone at the long oar, the calm captain in his tight, responsible cabin and the navigator who must find his course by chart or star, and the ordinary sea dog who lets out or pulls in sheets of sail, who chips the barnacles and the briny crust from the hull and deck, who drops or hauls in anchor while the ship heaves in port or lumbers in doldrums or scuds through storms.

He packed his valises. In some he stored the manuscripts intended for *La Décade Egyptienne* and a sheaf of Denon's drawings of hieroglyphics and monuments. He wrapped golden scraps and bibelots in little chamois pouches and stashed them in his green carrying case. And then, without drum or trumpet, Jean Lambert, as had his leader, found a boat and quit the scene.

X

Thérèse had granted him an interview. That was good for starters, thought Jean Lambert, because once she saw him and heard him and came to understand the extraordinary nature of his love for her, she would regain her senses or, more precisely, she would lose her senses and return to loving him again. There was also the special case of his one eye: who could fail to love a one-eyed man when he winked that eye and made it flutter madly?

The rich banker, Ouvrard, had made his money selling blankets to the revolutionary army. Thérèse's fellow jailbird friend, Rose, who had taken up her

new name, Josephine Bonaparte, with a force worthy
of her new husband's prestige, had put in a few good
words about Ouvrard's blankets to Barras, the de facto
head of the Directory, and soon the army were cover-
ing themselves with Ouvrard's thin, short-shrift strips
of blankets and were freezing off their skimpy asses
whenever they camped out in weather below 45°F.
Many soldiers froze to death in their sleep in the snowy
passage over the Alps during the Italian campaign.
Several officers grumbled about the poor heat-
retaining quality of Ouvrard's body covers, but their
complaints did not travel far, and even those which
reached Barras himself died at his boots without a
hearing.

Josephine received (without the General's knowledge) her commission for the sale of these blankets,
and Thérèse's future husband, Ouvrard, had en-
riched himself sufficiently to change his trade and deal,
much like an astronomer, with lofty figures rather than
with bolts of cloth and yards of blanket wool and the
problems of manufacturing and transporting and selling them. By the time Josephine introduced him
to Thérèse, Ouvrard had become the rich banker
Ouvrard, having brushed off every thread of his blankets, and was lending money to the government at
astronomical rates, his bookkeeping resembling the
calculations of the distance between stars.

Where were Robespierre and Saint-Just and the
rabid Hébert now, when he could have used them to

dispatch his rival—and a profiteering menace to the public—with one cut? Only Thérèse had the power to dislodge the banker from her life, and Jean Lambert's hopes of that were not tall. For the moment, the best he could expect was to be admitted to her parlor, from which platform he might stage his assault on her bedroom and there, under the canopy of embroidered stars, charge and recover lost ground. He was dizzy from such reflections, and by the time he reached her landing, he felt he had thought his way into a disadvantage. He would have turned and descended the stair but la señora Nuñez was prepared for him, having spied the pedestrian from the window ("Look! He's there, on foot!" la señora had cried out to her mistress as Tallien turned the corner), and she was ready at the door, which she pulled open at the sound of his last step.

Thérèse entered the parlor some minutes after la señora Nuñez (minus the Tricolor and red bonnet, and now wearing the stiff gray livery of a hall servant) had escorted her former employer to a comfortable settee. He had, in those minutes of waiting, the time to regard the Boucher and the Fragonard which once again hung on their familiar places on the wall, and to realize, suddenly, that he liked them. The Revolution had melted away from them and left them suspended in unpolemical loveliness. Louis Quinze's plump Irish whore lolled on her belly, her smile more naked than her pink, parted thighs. She was a joy. As she must have been to Boucher when he painted her in her royal keep that winter when kings and their pleasures were still sacrosanct.

"Well, madame," Jean Lambert began, rising from the settee. It was a sentence he never finished. He fell back to the seat like a brained calf, his hand shivering, his body shuddering in chills. A fever which had incubated in Egypt and was stewing in his blood through the weeks' voyage home swept through him at that instant, and in trying to speak he succeeded only in chattering his teeth. It was amusing, and he wanted Thérèse to see the joke of it, and he wanted her to pay attention to his fluttering eye, but she was rushing about, shouting instructions to rooms beyond, and at last some porters came and, half carrying him down the stairs, took him to the street and from there finally to his old attic room. Thérèse sent a physician to bleed him and to tend to him, but she herself never came, and as long as he lived, he never saw her again.

XI

Napoleon would not receive him. The First Consul had long forgotten Egypt, and he wished that others would have the grace never to remind him of what he had forgot. Thérèse, Jean Lambert conjectured, must have interceded for him with Josephine and she with the First Consul, because one day Tallien was notified he would be pensioned at half pay for the loss of his eye in the Italian campaign. A year passed before the pension began to trickle in. That was a normal delay, and Tallien was relieved that some definite means of income, however small, was assured him. He tried to repurchase some of the books he had sold from his collection, but they had either disappeared into private hands or had risen so astronomically in price as to be beyond his reach. One day the pension stopped materializing, disappearing as mysteriously as the miracle which had produced it.

And so, on sunny days when the green sap of trees yet sleeping sends its perfume along the thick blue river Seine, and on days when the sky shifts like wet dead gravel and rains down to the streets its gray showers, Jean Lambert's library went, book by book, to the open stalls and the booksellers' shops:

Sacrobosco, Johannes de. [John of Holywood.] *Tractatus de Sphaera Mundi.* [This is the second astronomical work to be printed.] Although recording no advance on the Arabian commentaries on Ptolemy, it won great reputation, twenty-four editions appearing before 1500. 4to. Original boards. Ferrara, 1472. [First edition.] Some foxing.

Lommius, Joost van. *Tableau des Maladies ou Description exacte de toutes les Maladies qui attaquent le Corps humain, avec leurs signes diagnostics & pronostics.* Paris. 1767. [12 mo. Contemp. mottled calf, top and bottom spine worn.]

The beast with two backs was selling for a song, for less even, for a few crooked bars of the "Marseillaise." Money was so tight and the weather so bad that Lucie-Marie and Sally, the chestnut vendor's daughter, had to peddle their asses extra hours, but in that cold even their usual customers couldn't get it up for them.

"I'd rather dip it into the Seine than stick it in that hairy tundra," shouted Marcel, the flour man, to a band of roving whores who, driven by the freeze, found themselves roaming in ever alien streets and unfamiliar parks.

Freezing sparrows perched stolidly on icy window-sills; nervous pigeons paddled about little frozen puddles along the quay. The winter was severe, the flats frozen, the streets cold-gray; beggars and the general poor crowded about crate fires in the open squares. Bundled men fished for eels through broken plates of the ice-sheeted Seine.

Through the month of the great freeze, Tallien dreamed of Egypt, her tombs and fiery sands, of the Pyramids on which soldiers of the Army of the Revolution had scratched their perishable names. He dreamed of when, after he had recovered from his illness on returning to Paris, he had sent Thérèse a pouch of golden scarabs.

But now she wouldn't even answer his letters. In one he reviled her infidelity, boasted of high positions that would be offered him shortly, that very hour. And in the same letter he begged her to intercede for him, to plead his case before Talleyrand (who could open doors bolted to the Pope), with whom he had learned she had dined a fortnight past. "All Paris knows he adores you and would favor my petition should you favor it. Let me be sent to Brazil; even to

FREDERIC TUTEN

live among marshes and monkeys is welcome. May I
tell my creditors you are arranging my safe-conduct
through these uncertain days? My God! I should
have let them take your head when I still had the
chance!"

This was followed by the last letter he was to write
her, a note actually, penned on the title page of his
Discours: "Thérèse, I am in want. Do you recall how
you had me confiscate several of Boulle's pieces from
the Pommard family, how you said you would suffer
should such magnificent objects fall into the hands of
the rampaging mobs and thus into their midnight
bonfires. Recall the *bonheur du jour*, the one inlaid
with marqueterie and edged with ebony and gold, the
one in whose little secret drawer you once kept my
letters? I ask only for that one. Keep the armoires,
the commodes, the cabinets, keep even the gilded
bureau mounted on brass lion's feet and set in blue
enamel."

Commerce had returned to optimum levels; expectations on the Bourse were high. But in the country-
side, peasants still hoarded grain and potatoes in
earthen cellars. Artists opened their studios to mer-
chants and their families. Portraits went by the square
foot, yet rates were negotiable, some barter tolerated.
Laces and silks, chambray and velvet returned to the
salons, although there was complete uncertainty as to
what was *de rigueur* for balls and late suppers: since
the Egyptian campaign, some detected an Oriental
trend, especially in the brocade slashing of evening

coats; and after the Peninsular War, a Spanish influence—several fashionable women wore castanets in
their hair—seemed to predominate, but neither mode
took hold.

Jean Lambert's life grew ever more solitary. No one
visited his tiny room, and there were few left for
him to visit. He was unknown in the new, smart cafés,
and he was on no one's invitation list. It was not that
doors were closed to him but that no one thought
of inviting him—he was not current news and had the
air of a relic of unholy times. Even so, should he have
been asked to a dinner or a party, he would have been
hard pressed to find a proper outfit. What clothes he
possessed were out of fashion, and worse, they were
threadbare and soiled. He stuffed cardboard in his
shoes and never thought to have them mended.

There were times he thought he would not outlast
the year. Stronger than his need for warm, suitable
clothes, than his daily hunger, was his loneliness. His
marrow felt lonely, that's how deeply it had pene-
trated him, he told himself. He had once believed himself adored by a beautiful woman and he had lived
passionately in the aura of her love (of greater meaning to him now than the Revolution and all its works),
but all that had been provisional, and now he was
left emptier than the spaces between the stars—his
own metaphor. At times he complained that destiny
had dealt him mocking cards, several rounds of full
houses and royal flushes, followed forever by empty
hands. It might have been better for him had the Revo-

lution never been born and he remained a printer's
apprentice and gone to the dogs in the way natural to
his class. What mattered now those honors and medals,
the handshake and salutation of the great, the knowledge of having helped divert, if only temporarily, the
stream of History, whose history was even presently
being revised by hostile pens? Jean Lambert thought
he now recognized the moral of the tale of the German
student he had read long ago. That while revolution
storms and ideas flood the field, the tide of your
psychic destiny pulls you more strongly than the pull
of ideas, and pulls you alone out to the open sea.

Beneath his window, carriages passed in the night,
bringing people to festivities, to brilliantly lit, warm,
capacious rooms. Once a barouche paused in the street
below. Jean Lambert's heart quickened. Perhaps it was
Thérèse, contrite, loving, finally come to rescue him
from his life. She would mount the stair, enter his
room—filling it with her radiance and warmth—
kneel before him, her eyes tear-brimmed. She would
say: "I have wronged you, my love. I have led a venal
life with soulless people. I want you, only you, forever you."

Joyously, they would reunite, recommencing the
great collaboration of their youth. But there was no
sound on the stair, no knock at the door, only the clat-
tering of hoofs, like dice rolling on a plate, and the
rumble of wheels as the carriage continued along its
way.

XII

Oh, Tallien! You in your cold bare room, you in the narrow bed and stiff, unchanged sheets, your sooty windows and molted dank walls, the fireplace cold, embers in the grate like the ashes of dead stars, you, Tallien, regicide and cuckold, the grinning wolf at your door, I watch you sortie out into the rue Bonaparte to hawk your early placards to a buying crowd ready for revolutionary souvenirs, and I think of restaging your story for modern life.

A music video for TV. We'll call your group Tallien and the Thermidorians—no, that's too fifties, maybe just the Terrorists. Your eighteenth-century weeds are wild enough for our times, so you don't have to change a thread, feel safe on that score. We'll get someone like Madonna to play Thérèse in hot pants and spike heels and black-leather bra. She'll flaunt her blond magic all over the set while you, in powdered wig and pastel-blue pantaloons, strut about with a quill, no, an ax in your hand, hacking off the heads of real-estate lords and arbitrage kings. Just in case someone complains, we can even throw in a welfare pimp for balance.

I am getting excited. This video could burn hotter than the sweaty porn shows of Batista's Havana, 1957, more electrifying than the currents in Pinochet's torture basements. You say you don't like it, you have to think it over. What's there to think? Who today will watch your sedate Rococo Dumb Show, do you imagine people are still going to silent films?

You want to keep your story closer to your own times; Fine. A solo number, maybe. That's good, too, just as long as you sing. Sing, you sanguine dandy, sing the song of the Blade and the blood-running streets, the regulation of the price of bread, the execution of the black marketeers and food hoarders, the masques of Reason at the guillotine steps; sing of Louis's gurgling head sliced into the blood-clotted basket. Above all, sing, you widower of the Revolution, the *chant d'amour* of when you first stuffed your radical cock into her perfumed sex—the first shot of the Year One.

—— ABOUT THE AUTHOR ——

FREDERIC TUTEN is the author of five novels: *The Adventures of Mao on the Long March; Tallien: A Brief Romance; Tintin in the New World; Van Gogh's Bad Café;* and most recently, *The Green Hour.*

He has written on art, film and literature for such publications as *Art Forum, Art in America,* and *The New York Times.* His short stories have appeared in *Tri-Quarterly, Fiction, The New Review of Literature, Fence, Conjunctions,* and *Granta.* He has published essays on the artists R.B. Kitaj, David Salle, Roy Litchtenstein, Eric Fischl, and John Baldessari.

For fifteen years, Dr. Tuten directed the Graduate Program in Literature and Creative Writing, which he helped found, at the City College of New York, where he is currently Professor Emeritus, and where he continues to conduct graduate seminars in fiction. He also conducts literature seminars at the New School University.

Tuten has received a Guggenheim Fellowship for Creative Writing and an Award for Distinguished Writing from the American Academy of Arts and Sciences.